THE
TE

DOCTOR WHO
THE TRIAL OF A TIME LORD:
TERROR OF THE VERVOIDS

based on the BBC television series by Pip and Jane Baker by
arrangement with BBC Books, a division of BBC Enterprises Ltd

PIP AND JANE BAKER

**Number 125 in the
Doctor Who Library**

A TARGET BOOK
published by
the Paperback Division of
W. H. ALLEN & Co. Plc

A Target Book
Published in 1988
by the Paperback Division of
W. H. Allen & Co. Plc
44 Hill Street, London W1X 8LB

The BBC producer of *The Vervoids* was John Nathan Turner,
the director was Chris Clough

The role of the Doctor was played by Colin Baker

Printed and bound in Great Britain by
Anchor Brendon Ltd, Tiptree, Essex

ISBN 0 426 20313 5

Prologue

At the apex of the cosmic evolutionary scale is the ultimate refinement of creation – a society comprised of Time Lords: beings whose intellectual prowess and agility surpass that of every other creature in the Universe. This facility has enabled them to develop the ability to travel in time. Past, present and future are all available to them: an awesome power.

Fortunately they are also gifted with moderating wisdom. A cardinal rule has become a pillar of the law that governs their conduct – they shall not meddle in the affairs of other societies. The penalty for transgression is death. An offender shall not only forfeit his or her life, but all remaining lives: for Time Lords can regenerate into a new personality when a current existence has run its course.

The Doctor is on trial.

Snatched out of time, he stands accused of this very crime. A vengeful prosecuting council, the Valeyard, has cited two cases as proof of his guilt. The Doctor has now to present evidence of his innocence.

1

The Defence Begins

A sombre hush permeated the Trial Room.

The Inquisitor in her white robes . . . the officiating Time Lords, veritable guardians of the Laws of Gallifrey . . . the black-garbed Valeyard . . . all watched the Doctor as he walked, leaden-footed, towards the prisoner's rostrum.

Gone was his usual ebullience.

Missing was his mischievous smile, his quirky eccentricity, as he mounted to the dock from where he was expected to submit the evidence that would either prove his innocence or confirm his guilt.

Yet, traumatic as this prospect might be, the Doctor's present despair was not for himself.

It was for Peri.

In the climax of the prosecutor's case, the Court had seen the Doctor allow his young companion to go to her doom.

'We are all aware of your feelings of sorrow, Doctor.' The Inquisitor's tone was gentle. 'Has the recess given you sufficient time to overcome the stress of your bereavement?'

The shock of Peri's death had so devastated the Doctor that he had been granted an adjournment. He lifted his uncharacteristically bowed head. 'I doubt if there will ever be sufficient time for that, my Lady.'

Although sensitive to his grief, the Inquisitor was also aware of the prosecutor's impatience. The Valeyard uttered an exaggerated sigh as the Doctor riffled through case notes, rubbed his brow, unable to focus despite the seriousness of the charge he faced.

The Court awaited his opening gambit.

None came.

Anxious to move in for the kill, the Valeyard rose. Head clamped in a black skull-cap, a stiff, silver-trimmed shoulder cape topping his voluminous black-as-night robes, he stretched to full height as his commanding tones shattered the silence. 'May we not proceed, my Lady?'

All attention switched to him.

'The cavalier manner in which the Doctor permitted his young and vulnerable companion to be destroyed militates against this charade of concern.'

A cruel statement. Yet true.

'The Doctor is fighting for his life, Valeyard,' reproved the Inquisitor. 'However, I take your point.'

Turning carefully so as not to disarrange the magnificent filigree halo-head-dress of white and gold or the wide stand-up collar that complemented it, she addressed the prisoner. 'Are you ready to present your evidence, Doctor?'

'Yes . . . Yes . . .' He raised his eyes, pools of sadness, to the huge screen behind the semi-circular tiers of seats where his peers sat in judgment.

'Like the prosecutor, I've utilised the Matrix in preparing my defence.' The Matrix, a link to the Amplified Panotropic Complex, was the computer that contained the memories of all the Time Lords that had ever existed. The screen was where those secrets could be viewed.

'My excursion will be into the future.' There was none of his usual swashbuckling in the Doctor's manner as he surveyed the assembly.

'The future?' The Valeyard's scepticism was not disguised. 'Is it to be the Doctor's defence that he improves?'

7

'Precisely.'

'This I must see!' The Valeyard sat down, arms folded in a seeming mood of resignation – that was belied by the assiduous keenness with which he turned to the blank Matrix screen.

'My submission involves a crisis that threatens not only the lives of a group confined together with no means of escape, but would, if unresolved, menace every mortal being on the planet Earth.'

The Doctor's statement brought a rustle of expectation from the elderly Time Lords.

'Proceed, Doctor.' The Inquisitor swung her chair round to face the screen.

'Perhaps with a little less hyperbole . . .' Sarcasm came naturally to the Valeyard. He never missed an opportunity for a gibe. The Doctor's demise was his mission and he intended to achieve it. No matter how.

Bracing himself, still trying to shed the vestiges of remorse for Peri's death, the Doctor pressed the button that activated the Matrix.

Onto the screen blinked the curved horizon of a planet shrouded in languidly swirling gases, tinged with cadmium yellow and orange.

'This is Mogar,' the Doctor explained. 'An oxygen-free planet in the Perseus Arm of the Milky Way. A rich source of rare metals.'

A multi-decked spaceship with the name *Hyperion III* emblazoned on its hull came into view. It was an intergalactic liner that ferried between Mogar and Earth. A scheduled flight in the Earth year 2986.

'A top priority consignment of these precious metals is being loaded aboard the *Hyperion III*.' Small craft shuttled from the planet to the massive, stationary spaceship.

All concentration was on the screen as the scene changed from outside the space liner to inside.

A winding, open staircase corkscrewed its way down into a capacious lounge elegantly furnished with white tables and white intricately-carved chairs. Crew members, smartly dressed in white uniforms, moved across the lounge, tending to the passengers' needs. Others descended the spiral staircase, carrying baggage.

'The crew await the last passengers as they prepare for an apparently routine voyage,' continued the Doctor.

The slight emphasis on 'apparently' did not escape the listeners in the Court.

Tersely, the Doctor went on. 'Many will never complete the journey.'

In the lounge, an elderly man lowered himself gingerly into an ornate chair. Two strangely-attired aliens padded past him. Sheathed from top to toe in skin-tight silver suits, their heads were completely encased in helmets. They were Mogarians. One, Atza, was talking rapidly to his companion, Ortezo, but the conversation was unintelligible to the rest of the passengers. And, indeed, to the occupants of the Trial Room.

Two more arrivals, Bruchner and Doland, reported in to the pert stewardess, Janet, before the Doctor dropped his final bombshell.

'Many will die . . . For in order to protect a secret hidden on the space liner, one of them will become a murderer . . .'

*   *   *

As the Doctor's words echoed around the Trial Room, another voice, strident and commanding, emanated from the screen.

'Am I expected to trust my life for heaven knows how many miles to a bunch of incompetents who cannot even get my luggage aboard without losing it!'

All this was said with no pause for breath and in ear-splitting decibels that fractured the calm of the thirtieth-century lounge. This was Professor Lasky. Blonde, in her forties, her trim figure draped in a puce trouser suit with matching waist-length cape, she strode from the entrance to the passenger cabins towards Janet at the reception desk.

Janet, her blush enhancing the pink trimmings on her short, neat, white uniform, hastily consulted her clipboard. 'Your luggage, Professor? It's not in your cabin?'

'Really? Do I have to repeat myself!'

The discomfited stewardess winced, but stood her ground. 'I'm sure we can sort it out –'

'Problems, Janet?' The question came from an officer with thinning hair and an ingratiating manner. 'Let me help.'

'And who are you?' Despite his badges of seniority, Lasky treated him like a menial cadet.

'Security Officer Rudge, Professor. Which cabin did you go to?'

'You're asking? And you're the Security Officer?' Her incredulity caused him to bestow a benevolent smile. Rudge was an avuncular individual who punctured his own authority by indecisiveness at crucial moments: a man promoted once too often.

It had not taken Lasky long to sum him up. 'Cabin Six!' she bawled. 'Where else?'

'May I see your key?' His smile did not waver as, with bad grace, she thrust the key at him.

He studied the tag. 'Ah . . . no . . . the other way round, I think.' He offered the key with the tag showing Nine instead of Six. '*You're* in Cabin Nine, Professor. And that's where your luggage will be.'

'Let's hope so!' Not in the least abashed, Lasky

10

stalked away to join her two assistants, Bruchner and Doland.

A new arrival approached Janet. She accepted his ticket and consulted her clipboard. With a side glance at Professor Lasky, she handed the key to the robust, good-looking newcomer whose hair and beard had gone prematurely grey. '*You're* in Cabin Six, Mister Grenville.'

Grenville grinned wryly and, pocketing his key, crossed to the exit marked *CABINS*. As he did so, the elderly man rose from his chair.

'Mister Hallet!' The old man's wizened features broke into a smile of pleasure. He advanced on Grenville, hand outstretched in welcome. 'How pleasant! At least one face not belonging to a stranger.'

Ignoring the proffered hand, Grenville tried to pass. 'I'm sorry. I think you must be mistaken.'

'Surely not? My name's Kimber. We met three years ago. On Stella Stora. You came to investigate shortages in the granaries, Mister Hallet.'

Suddenly all attention was on the encounter. The opaque goggles of the Mogarians, Atza and Ortezo, were blatantly fixed on Grenville. So, too, was the attention of Lasky and her acolytes, Bruchner and Doland.

'I've never been to Stella Stora,' insisted the man Kimber had called Hallet. 'And my name's Grenville. You're obviously confusing me with someone else.' He continued to the cabins.

The elderly gentleman smoothed his balding pate, thoroughly confused.

'Maybe Mister Grenville has a *Doppelgänger*!' Rudge had been an interested spectator. So had Janet.

'I could have sworn . . . the face . . . even the voice sounds the same . . .'

As the door closed behind Grenville, the tall, thin

11

Bruchner turned to his associates. 'An investigator! Did you hear what –'

'*Bruchner!*' Lasky's reprimand was quiet but authoritative. 'Go and check the safety measures for the isolation room.'

Bruchner, aware he was being told to shut up, nevertheless was too agitated to obey.

'*Immediately!*'

Reluctantly, he departed. Lasky and Doland watched him go, then exchanged a glance of mutual concern. The Mogarians conversed in agitated whispers. Rudge gazed thoughtfully at the still swinging exit door. Janet, her duties forgotten, stared absently at her passenger list.

The apparently irrelevant mistaken identity seemed to have unnerved more than the elderly Mister Kimber . . .

2

Identity Crisis

Grenville, too, had lost his cool. Entering Cabin Six, he slung his case on the bed in obvious anger and frustration. Encountering old Mister Kimber had been a major blow.

He slumped onto the bed, glared around the simply furnished cabin. Neither the wardrobe nor the *en suite* bathroom offered inspiration.

But he had to do something!

Listening to ensure no-one was in the corridor, he stole out of the cabin.

'Come on! Move it!'

In contrast with the guard's staccato orders, the muted heartbeat of the idling engines throbbed rhythmically through the tenebrous cargo bay.

From a vantage point on a gantry high up in the shadows of latticed pipes and girders, Grenville watched the hive of activity below: loaders, in grey overalls, were trundling cargo into the vast hold.

'Keep it moving, lads. Keep it moving!'

Surreptitiously, Grenville surveyed the cavernous bay stacked with multifarious packing cases and crates . . . then he focused his gaze on a row of hooks from which hung overalls, identical to those worn by the loaders.

Officiously, the guard checked the manifest handed to him by the foreman. This diversion provided Grenville with the opportunity he sought. Stealthily descending the iron ladder, he made for the row of hooks.

'That's the final batch,' confirmed the guard. 'Get your men ashore.'

Trooping towards the exit, the loaders yanked hoods with masks attached over their heads: the air on Mogar was as lethal to humans as the oxygenated air on the ship was to the two Mogarian passengers on board.

Quickly donning a pair of overalls, Grenville pulled the hood over his head and, anonymity assured, filed from the ship with the disembarking men.

*   *   *

Intriguing as this action was to the rest of the court, the Valeyard had an objection.

'Relevant, I hope,' cautioned the Inquisitor.

'Completely. When, may we ask, is the Doctor going to embroil himself in this saga?'

'Now *I* object!' The Doctor felt extremely angry. 'Am I not to be protected from the prosecutor's insinuations? On what evidence does he conclude that I embroil myself?'

'None.' The Inquisitor's smooth features registered no surprise at the Doctor's outburst. 'I shall ignore his terminology. But I confess I share his curiosity.'

'I fail to see why you are curious, my Lady. You must be aware of where the TARDIS is.' The sarcasm was barely hidden. That the TARDIS had been 'bugged' was something he had learned from the earlier prosecution case. Chagrin had hit him then. Now he could not resist the barbed rejoinder.

'Obscurity is a recognised ploy for subterfuge,' sneered the Valeyard.

'And posing unnecessary questions in order to score cheap points is the ploy used by a prosecutor who has no case!' countered the Doctor. 'You've been monitoring the TARDIS! You claim it's been bugged with a listening device! So – you tell the Court where it is!'

Awaiting the prosecutor's response, the Inquisitor straightened the crimson sash draped across her white robes. 'I require you to respond to the challenge, Valeyard.'

The Valeyard dared not disobey her. 'It had entered the sector the *Hyperion III* is traversing.' His reluctance added to the Doctor's triumph as, with evident anticipation, all turned to the Matrix screen . . .

*   *   *

Against a backcloth of distant stars, galaxies and cosmic dust, the streamlined, multi-decked *Hyperion III* surged away from the planet of Mogar and hurtled through space . . .

. . . yet inside, no tremor of movement could be felt. No sound of the hyperon particle thruster engines could be heard.

So smooth was the lift-off that not a drop of coffee slurped over the brim of the beaker Janet was taking to the crew's quarters.

In a sudden, prancing gesture, a gloved fist seized her shoulder.

'Oh, you startled me!'

Ignoring her bewilderment, the Mogarian, Atza, began speaking. An unintelligible, guttural voice was broadcast from an electronic box linked by a nozzle to his begoggled helmet.

'You haven't got your translator switched on, sir.'

Impatiently, Atza jabbed a stud on the electronic box. 'Why did we not depart on schedule?' he asked.

Quickly regaining her equilibrium, Janet became the calm stewardess again. 'We were delayed for a late arrival. Gentleman from your planet, as a matter of fact.'

'A Mogarian?'

'Yes, sir!'

Abruptly, Atza departed. With a shrug, Janet continued along the corridor.

Another disconcerting happening was taking place in the communications room.

Seated before a sophisticated bank of audio and visual transmitters, Edwardes, the twenty-five-year-old Communications Officer, was frowning as he studied a monitor screen.

The object of his concern was a minute graphic glowing on the screen's North East quadrant.

'What the blazes can it be?' he muttered to himself. He had already consulted the flight log and found no notification of other spacecraft. Nor did the graphic conform to any vehicle in the Space Mariners' Manual.

Nor would it. For the object was the Doctor's TARDIS.

Unaware of his proximity to the liner – indeed, oblivious of anything but the bouncy, red-haired young woman supervising his programme, the Doctor was pedalling furiously on an exercise bike.

The girl was Mel, his new companion. And instructress!

'Twenty . . . twenty-one . . . twenty-two . . .' She and the Doctor counted together: he with martyr-like resignation, she with bubbling vitality.

'Twenty-three . . . twenty-four . . .'

Still counting in unison with her reluctant pupil, Mel trotted from the control room.

The instant she was out of sight, the Doctor stopped pedalling but continued counting vigorously.

'Twenty-five . . . twenty-six . . . twenty-seven . . .' His contribution was even more emphatic as he slumped over the handlebars – then hastily resumed dedicated action on her return: 'twenty-eight . . . twenty-nine . . . thirty!' He collapsed forward.

'Here, this'll buck you up.' She was carrying two glasses.

The Doctor eyed the orange liquid in the glasses disgustedly. 'Carrot juice!'

'It'll do you good, honestly. Carrots are full of Vitamin A.'

Disingenuously, the Doctor fingered his ears. 'Mel . . . have you studied my ears lately?'

'It's your waistline I'm concerned about.' Mel, who had been with the Doctor for three months, had already learnt to recognise his wily deceptions.

'No, seriously, is it my imagination' – he stroked imaginary donkey-length ears through his mop of fair curls – 'or are they growing longer?'

Mel, brown eyes twinkling, was not taken in. 'Listen, when I start calling you Neddy, then you can worry! Drink up!'

'You'll worry sooner if I start to bray!'

Grinning, Mel swigged her carrot juice and he, with good-humoured reluctance, took a minute sip. . . .

The persistence of the twenty-two-year-old Mel was matched by the Communications Officer on the *Hyperion III*.

Trying to make sense of the glowing graphic, Edwardes was coding in signal sequences on a touch-sensitive keyboard.

His efforts went unrewarded. Despite his considerable skills, he could not find a channel that would allow him to establish contact with the strange object.

So baffled was he, that he failed to look round when Janet entered with refreshments.

Putting down the tray, she joined him at the console. 'Anything interesting?'

'Maybe. Unidentified craft. I've tried all the standard frequencies.'

'Without response?'

'Not a bleep.' Taking the beaker, he tasted his coffee.

'Perhaps it's a piece of space flotsam.'

With amused condescension, Edwardes gazed at his earnest colleague. 'You make delicious coffee, Janet.'

'Oh well, if you don't want the benefit of my advice . . .' Her haughtiness was all pretence as she flounced from the room.

A smile creasing his pleasant features, Edwardes resumed his signalling. 'Let's try you on hyper-frequency.'

He tapped out a code. Waited eagerly for a response. When none came, he tried again . . . Absorbed in his task, he did not see the door handle turning . . . or hear the soft footsteps of an intruder . . .

The first awareness hit him when the flat disc of a high-pressure syringe stabbed against his jugular . . . Edwardes' cry of protest was stillborn. Coffee splattering, he slumped forward, unconscious . . .

The intruder had not finished.

Gloved hands reached for the touch-sensitive keyboard and began tapping out a message . . .

3

Welcome Aboard

Exhausted, feet strapped to the bike's motionless pedals, the Doctor was watching the tireless Mel. Her rope slapped with clockwork regularity against the floor as she blithely reached ninety-seven in her daily dose of a hundred skips. A signal began bleeping on the control panel.

'Quick, Mel, press the red button! Get the message on the screen!'

Mel pressed the red button but the screen remained blank.

'Press it, girl! Press it!'

'I have.'

Awkwardly struggling free of the straps, he rushed to the console and thumped a green button.

'You said red!' Mel was indignant.

'Did I? It's the carrot juice making me colour blind!'

A sequence of numbers flickered onto the monitor.

'Colour blind!' Mel looked disparagingly at her companion's variegated costume.

The Doctor ignored the jibe. His concentration was on concurrently translating the numbers into letters as the message continued.

The bleeping ceased.

Decoded, the message read: '– *PERATIVE TRAITOR BE IDENTIFIED BEFORE LANDING EARTH. MAYDAY END.*

'Cryptic,' was the Doctor's comment.

'Mayday call. We have to respond.'

He didn't need Mel to tell him that. He had already set the co-ordinates. 'Practically on our doorstep!'

With a wheezing bellowing and a flashing light, the familiar police box, otherwise known as the TARDIS, materialised in the sombrely-lit hold of the *Hyperion III*.

Mel's mass of red curls jutted from the door. 'Come on, Doctor. Come on. Hurry.'

She stepped impetuously into the deserted gloom, eyeing the crates and packages.

'How I've kept up with you these last three months is a constant source of wonder to me!'

'No-one sends a Mayday unless it's a matter of life and death.' Mel's piping tones echoed round the enormous void.

'Yes, well let's exercise the little grey cells instead of the muscles for once, shall we?'

A wise precaution although he did not realise how wise at that moment, for he had not spotted a figure darting through the stacks of cargo.

'This wasn't an ordinary call. It was beamed specifically to the TARDIS.' No simple feat. Contact with the TARDIS communicator could not be made fortuitously.

'So it was from somebody who knows you,' stated Mel.

Another figure, still unseen by Mel and the Doctor, sprinted between the crates.

'Then why wasn't it signed?'

'Panic. Desperation. We won't find out by hanging about in here, will we?' Once Mel got the bit between her teeth she was unstoppable! She was no wilting flower, despite being only four feet ten without her high-heeled boots and as slim as a willow in her cream pants-suit.

'We won't go blundering into a trap either!'

'I've never seen this side of you before. You're the one who usually charges in regardless.'

Certainly the Doctor seemed reluctant to proceed. He squinted towards a section cordoned off behind a mesh fence. 'Can't you sense it, Mel?'

'Sense what?'

'Evil. There's evil in this place.' He retreated to the TARDIS. 'I have a better suggestion. We'll go to –'

'Doctor!' The barrel of a phaser was levelled at Mel's temple by a maroon-uniformed guard.

'-Pyro Shika.' The Doctor had not interrupted his flow of thought or looked round. 'A fascinating planet with –'

'Doctor!'

This time he could not ignore Mel's cry of alarm because a phaser was now poking into his spine! The two sinister figures had been guards on duty. Mel and the Doctor had become their captives.

'So much for your enthusiasm!' The Doctor whispered to Mel. 'Let me do the talking!' Mustering what was meant to be an innocent and beguiling smile, he cajoled the guard. 'Now, listen, my man, I can explain –'

'Shut up! Move!' He matched the instruction with a sharp prod.

Mel, frightened but not intimidated, reproved the Doctor. 'You certainly talked us out of trouble there!'

Touché. Having no adequate response, the Doctor, thrust by the intractable guard, stumbled towards the door.

From deeper within the shadowy bowels of the hold, a third figure had witnessed the arrival and capture of the Doctor and Mel.

Unlike the guards, he was enveloped in a silver, skin-tight suit and helmet. Another Mogarian – the late

21

boarder the stewardess had mentioned. He was distinguished from his compatriots by a gold sash. Like them, his name ended in a vowel and contained a 'z': he was called Enzu.

Alone, he abandoned his hiding place and strode to the cordoned-off sector. Bathed in a suffused ochre glow, it was difficult to identify what lay behind the closely-meshed fence. A notice attached to the locked gate read:

HIGH INTENSITY LIGHT FORBIDDEN.
LOW SPECTRUM LIGHT ONLY.

After a cursory inspection of the palm-print-recognition lock, Enzu directed his attention to the tungsten links clinching the mesh fence to a post.

'You never heard anything?'

Unaware that a burglary was underway, and two intruders had joined the ship's company, Security Officer Rudge was quizzing the drug-confused Edwardes on the bridge.

'Not a sound.'

'Nor saw anything?'

'I've already told you.'

'No-one's blaming you, laddie. But I thought perhaps now your head's clearer . . .'

'I was concentrating on the unidentified craft.'

'From which you failed to get a response.'

Suppressing a sigh of irritation, the Commodore intervened. 'Mister Edwardes, what about the tape?' Unlike Rudge, the Commodore was a man who exuded authority. Grey-haired, clean shaven, immaculately groomed, his dark eyes barely concealed the growing impatience with which he was witnessing his subordinate's bumbling debriefing of the Communications Officer.

Edwardes' attitude underwent a change. 'De-

22

activated, sir.'

'Which indicates knowledge of our procedures.' A clue to the attacker's identity. But a slim one. It meant only that he or she knew that all messages sent or received were automatically monitored and taped.

'Just my thoughts too, Commodore.' Rudge could sense the initiative slipping away from him.

'I'm sure.' The emphasis left no-one in doubt as to the Commodore's estimation of Rudge. Including Rudge himself.

'How about the rest of the equipment?'

'In perfect order, sir.' Deference now from Edwardes.

'That leaves only one objective your assailant could have had.'

'To send a message.' Rudge's attempt to get back into the driving seat received a peremptory rebuff.

'I was trying not to state the obvious, Mister Rudge.' Dismissively, the Commodore swung his chair to face the command console beyond which he could see, through a wall-to-ceiling window, the endless horizon of star-dappled space. 'Report to the Medic before returning to duty, Edwardes.'

'Thank you, sir –'

'Will you stop poking that contraption into my spine!'

It was the Doctor's voice. He and Mel were being unceremoniously shunted onto the bridge by the guards.

Instead of leaving, Edwardes lingered, casting an appreciative glance at the attractive Mel.

'We heard a noise in the cargo hold, Mister Rudge,' one of the guards began to explain, 'and found these two –'

'Is it?' Completely ignoring the guard, the Doctor advanced, hand outstretched, on the Commodore. 'Yes, it is! Captain Travers!'

The proffered hand was assiduously ignored as the Commodore eyed the Doctor. 'Commodore.' He patently did not share the Time Lord's delight at renewing an acquaintanceship. 'Of all the places in this infinite Universe, you have to turn up on my ship!'

'Commodore? Then we must be on a Grade One Security Craft.'

'And *I'd* like to know how you got here!' Feeling the business of dealing with stowaways was his department, Rudge attempted to assume the role of interrogator.

It was a wasted effort. 'Don't bother, Rudge. *I* know how. What I don't know is why!'

'Didn't you signal us?'

'Me!' The Commodore's tone left little doubt that the Doctor would be the last person he'd signal!

'A Mayday call. We had to respond.' Mel had been silent for long enough. It was not in her nature to be passive.

Edwardes, obviously taken with the vivacious redhead, and conscious that his superior officer operated on a very short fuse, leapt to her support. 'That's true, sir.'

He received a snub for his pains. 'I'm fully conversant with the Navigational Code, Mister Edwardes. I thought you were reporting to the Medic.'

'Er – yes – sir.' With a tentative smile at Mel, he hurried off.

The Commodore had not finished with castigating the Doctor. 'I authorised no Mayday signal.'

The Time Lord's shrug did nothing to allay his suspicion.

'My Communication Officer's attacked – then *you* appear!'

'And a fat lot of thanks we've got for our pains!' Mel wasn't prepared to let anyone ride roughshod over her or the Doctor.

'If I seem to lack gratitude, young woman –'

24

'Melanie, known as Mel,' interjected the Doctor.

'– it is because on the previous occasion the Doctor's path crossed mine, I found myself involved in a web of mayhem and intrigue!'

'I saved your ship, Commodore.'

'Yes, you did. Though whether it would have been at risk without your intervention is another matter.'

'Whatever happened in the past doesn't alter the fact that a Mayday call was sent.' Like her plans for slimming down the Doctor, Mel never gave up, once committed.

The Time Lord was prepared to. 'But – not sent by you, Commodore. So let's make this hail and farewell.'

'Stand easy, Doctor!' No compromise in the Commodore's tone. 'You're not leaving.'

'We're not?'

'I'd rather have you where I can see you than swanning around outside.' He addressed the guard. 'Conduct them to the lounge.' A final order to the visiting pair. 'Consider yourselves restricted to the passenger quarters.'

Mel resented the dictatorial manner. 'In other words, welcome aboard.'

Unable to suppress a small grin at her cheeky parting crack, the Commodore swung his command chair about in order to study the longitude and latitude grid superimposed on the navigational window.

'Stowaways! I could've done without that on my final service report.' Rudge's comment was addressed to the Commodore's back.

'If you're expecting an easy ride on your last voyage, Mister, I'm afraid you're not going to get it!' The Commodore had no doubts about the trouble potential of the Time Lord.

'I think you're being a mite unfair, sir,' bleated Rudge.

'Am I? Well, don't be too diligent in policing the

Doctor.'

'Can I have clarification of that instruction, sir?'

'Give him enough rope – and he'll snare our culprit for us.'

The Commodore knew the Doctor well!

The Commodore might have been less sanguine, however, had he known of Enzu's activities.

Having breached the wire mesh, the Mogarian discovered what appeared to be a hydroponic centre dominated by giant plants. Two metres in height and almost a metre in diameter, the tall sentinels were pod-shaped with dark-green, leafy exteriors.

Giving the freakish plants a wide berth, Ensu entered a small hut and switched on the light.

This was no gardener's potting shed. It contained scientific apparatus, test-tubes, balances and pipettes.

All of this received only a perfunctory glance. Enzu's interest was in the rows of jars, each containing a collection of seeds. He unscrewed the jar labelled *DEMETER* and tipped its contents onto his palm. The silver, bean-shaped seeds were like none he had ever seen before.

Had he glanced through the open door, he would have seen an even more intriguing sight. The beam of light streaming from the hut had illuminated a giant pod. No longer lulled by the soft, ochre, low spectrum light, bathed instead in the ray of harsh, high spectrum white, the pod had begun to pulsate gently . . .

The seeds clasped in his gloved hand, Enzu replaced the jar and quit the hut.

The beam of light was immediately extinguished . . . the pulsating of the awakened pod subsided . . .

But for how long?

Had Enzu unwittingly begun a process that could not be halted?

4

Limbering Up

Travelling as a passenger was an unusual experience for the Doctor. He was used to being master of his own destiny.

Ensconced in a chair, feet up on another, he seemed to have accepted his role. Janet was circulating among other guests in the lounge, offering refreshments. When she approached him, he reached for a couple of chocolate biscuits – Mel vetoed that!

Sighing, he allowed the inviting delicacies to pass. The disappointed glare he gave his slim, young companion was soon superseded by genuine concern. After all, she was virtually a prisoner.

'Not quite the carefree life of Pease Pottage, Sussex, Mel.'

'Have you heard me complaining?'

He mustered a weak smile that did not convince her. 'You're really worried, aren't you?' she asked.

'I can't rid myself of the feeling I'm being manipulated. Whoever sent that signal knew me.'

Ever the pragmatist, Mel had a ready solution. 'There's a made-to-measure candidate.'

'There is?'

'The Commodore. He's met you before.'

'He'd've said.'

'Would he? Admit he needs outside assistance!'

'An intriguing possibility. But that's all.'

Enzu entered the lounge. Nothing in his demeanour gave any hint of his earlier pilfering in the hydroponic

27

centre. Nor did the Doctor show any but a transient interest as Enzu settled down at a nearby VDU.

Mel's reaction was simply to lower her voice. 'Look, the quickest way out of this is to solve the mystery.'

Ostensibly deeply absorbed in the novel she was reading, Lasky noisily turned a page.

'That could also be the quickest way into trouble.' Was the Doctor as indifferent to the activity around him as he appeared to be?

Mel did not deviate from her theme. 'Why don't you ask for the passenger list?'

'Don't hustle me, Mel.'

'Who's hustling? All I'm saying is you might recognise a name. Simple, isn't it?'

Her plans for occupying the Doctor roused his suspicions. 'Meanwhile?'

'Meanwhile, I go for a wander. Poke my nose into the nooks and crannies and see if anyone tries to make contact. Remember,' she said, rising, 'we were restricted to the passenger quarters.' A mischievous grin. 'This is only the lounge . . .'

Glad to be taking some action, she stepped spritely for the exit.

Did the Doctor, still reclining lazily, notice the opaque goggles of Enzu following Mel's progress?

If he did, he gave no sign.

Somebody else was interested in Mel's progress, too.

In the deserted corridor, she was trying the door of the nearest cabin when she heard footsteps. She scampered to where there was a plan of the ship's interior fixed to the wall.

The pursuer was Rudge.

'Looking for something, Miss?' His pose was overtly polite but beneath their pale lashes his eyes regarded her sceptically.

'Er – I see you've a gymnasium.' Quick thinking on Mel's part.

'Need it on a long trip like this.' He was equal to the subterfuge.

'Thought I might do a bit of limbering up.'

'That's the spirit. I'll take you there.' The perfect ship's officer, anxious to keep the passengers happy!

A reasonable assumption.

Not for Mel. She was blunt. 'So you can keep tabs on me?'

Rudge's polite smile widened into a grin. 'Now, Miss,' he chuckled. 'Why would I want to do that?'

With a diplomatic indication in the direction of the gym, he escorted her along the corridor.

Another polite manoeuvre was taking place. In the lounge.

Mustering all his charm, the Doctor approached Janet. 'I wonder if you can help me?'

'I'll do my best.'

'I'd like a copy of the passenger list.'

The 'professional hostess' expression on Janet's pretty face flickered with disquiet. Fleetingly. She was soon back in control. 'A copy of the passenger list, Doctor?'

'Yes.' He had not missed the sudden impromptu reaction. 'Can you get it for me?'

A sentry yawned expansively. He had been on duty outside a cabin marked *ISOLATION ROOM* for three hours. Relief was due in thirty minutes but boredom was stretching those thirty minutes into an eternity.

An abrupt stiffening to attention. The tall, thin Bruchner, his narrow vulpine face made to seem even longer by receding hair, was hurrying along the corridor carrying a kidney dish, swabs and syringes.

Brusquely, he motioned the sentry aside. Then, pulling the surgical mask, already dangling under his chin, up over his mouth and nose, he entered the isolation room.

The sentry's orders were to allow only Professor Lasky and her two colleagues to pass. But he was puzzled. Bruchner was an agronomist. The study of plants was his work. Yet here he was, masquerading with all the trappings of a doctor. For besides the surgical mask, he wore the ankle-length protective gown of a surgeon about to perform a delicate operation . . .

Bruchner's superior, Professor Lasky, was putting herself through torture on a spine-stretching rack in the gym.

Her handsome features contorted in agony, the eminent scientist was vehemently subjecting herself to the routine she had evolved to keep her fit during the long and sedentary journey. The blonde head continued to bob up and down without a pause as Mel entered.

Following instructions already issued by Rudge, Mel unhooked a headset from the collection hanging from a shelf, and slipped it on.

A blast of aerobic music accosted her eardrums!

'Sorry, Miss.' Rudge, in the observation cubicle, was looking through the narrow dormer window that presented a view into the gym.

His apology was patently insincere as he adjusted the volume on the audio deck which occupied most of the cubicle. The rest of the small antechamber consisted of shelves crammed with labelled instruction tapes covering every type of exercise and keep-fit routine any space traveller could acquire.

He spoke into the microphone. 'If you get tired of

aerobics, just select another tape. They're all complete with instructions and music.'

Leaving Mel to limber into a programme of lithe gyrations, he returned into the corridor, almost colliding with Doland who was scurrying towards the gym.

Less tall than Bruchner and more stockily built, Doland had a mane of thick, wavy hair framing his sallow complexion. Usually imperturbable, his behaviour now was quite the opposite.

'We've got a problem, Professor! In the hydroponic centre!' So intense was his alarm that his normally low-keyed voice was raised several decibels.

Lasky's booming tones matched his. 'The hydroponic centre! What's happened?'

Doland's distraught behaviour caused Mel to lift an earphone to listen. He caught the action and waited for her to replace it before he continued.

'It's been broken into!'

Without hesitation, Lasky dismounted from the rack. 'Get Bruchner down there!' She was already stalking from the gym. 'He's in the isolation room.'

Intrigued, Mel watched their agitated departure.

So did somebody in the audio cubicle . . .

As the doors swung to behind the agronomists, the observer began towards the gym – then stopped as another passenger, unaware of the drama, entered to get her daily dose of suntan from the vionesium sunlamp.

Frustrated, the observer picked up the mike and flicked the switch that would connect with Mel's headset and override the music.

'Who's speaking?' Mel's expression changed as the unfamiliar voice whispered into her headset. 'Yes. Yes, I heard, but who are you?'

Receiving no reply, Mel whipped off the headset and, in a whirlwind of arms and legs, dashed into the cubicle.

No-one.

Elbowing through the door, she peered along the corridor.

Deserted too.

In determined strides, Mel made for the lounge.

She did not know who had spoken.

She did not recognise the voice.

What she did realise was that the message the voice had uttered must be relayed to the Doctor immediately.

5

Tiger Trap

No longer wearing his surgical mask and gown, Bruchner bustled into the cargo hold in the wake of Lasky and Doland.

Lasky stormed to the hydroponic centre, halting at the mesh fence. A hole big enough to permit access had been forced. 'You appalling dunderhead, Doland! Couldn't you have repaired this?'

Although Lasky was the charismatic leader of the scientific team, her abrasive reprimand incited resentment in the equally well-qualified Doland. But he was a man of restraint whose feelings did not easily surface.

'I assumed you wanted to see the damage for yourself.' His pique was tempered with deference.

Sarah Lasky was not prepared to be placated. 'And I suppose it never penetrated your thick academic skull to check the pods?'

It had. That was the first thing he had done on discovering the violated mesh. 'They're stable,' he asserted.

Even so, she plunged into the dank growing-area, her angry features jaundice-hued by the ochre low spectrum light.

In the eerie glow, the tall plants remained broodingly dormant. There was no evidence of the pulsating prompted earlier by the shaft of white light. Nothing to indicate that it had ever happened. The sole movement was the liquid gurgling through transparent feeder-tubes.

'Professor Lasky!' It was Bruchner calling urgently. Anxious to avoid the verbal flack his colleague was suffering Bruchner had gone directly to the work hut where he had found the empty seed jar.

'The Demeter seeds, Professor! They've gone!'

Puzzlement rather than alarm was the reaction of the three agronomists as they gazed at the empty jar . . .

Racing along the corridor towards the lounge, Mel had forgotten all about Lasky's and Doland's strange behaviour in the gym. Only the relayed message was on her mind. And the need to deliver it to the Doctor.

He, meanwhile, was engaged on other matters: subjecting Janet to his beguiling wiles.

'You're very persuasive, Doctor, but I can't possibly – ah, here's the man who could give you permission.'

Rudge had entered the lounge.

Rudge! The Doctor had no desire to join combat with the Security Officer. 'No, no. Don't bother –'

Too late!

'Permission for what?' asked Rudge.

'It's not important. A mere whim. I'm subject to whims. So I'm told.'

'The Doctor wants a passenger list.' Janet supplied the answer.

A sheepish grin quivered on the Time Lord's lips as he prepared for the inevitable chastisement.

None came. Instead: 'Why not? Indeed the idea makes good sense.' Examining the Doctor through half-closed lids, Rudge offered the clipboard.

'If I could spot a familiar name . . .' faltered the Time Lord lamely, skimming through the list.

'We'd have our culprit' – Rudge intervened unctuously – 'And you'd be bidding us farewell. Should've thought of that myself. Sign of age. Due to retire after this trip.'

Diminutive she might be, but Mel's entrance into the lounge would have done credit to a small posse of wilde-beest! Not only the Doctor but every other occupant glanced up as she clattered in.

'Er . . . no . . . no . . . Complete strangers, I'm afraid.' The Doctor returned the clipboard.

'Pity!' Rudge sounded sincere.

'Many thanks.' With affected indifference, the Doctor sauntered across the lounge to his keyed-up companion.

Conscious that the security officer was watching them, Mel spoke quietly but urgently. 'He's been in touch. He wants you to meet him in Cabin Six!'

'Did you see him? Get a name?'

'No, just a message through my headphones when I was in the gym. Let's go!'

She was about to move when the Doctor stopped her. 'Mel, before you rush off, d'you know what a Judas goat is?'

'Um – er – yes, a decoy goat that's tied to a stake to lure the tiger into the open.'

'Getting badly mutilated in the process. I think I shall refuse the role.' He began to mount the spiral staircase.

'Then where are you going?'

'For a non-provocative stroll around the deck.'

'What about Cabin Six?'

'Tiger trap!'

Tiger trap indeed. For Cabin Six was a shambles. The scene of a tremendous struggle. Sheets and pillows were strewn about the floor. Clothes torn from the wardrobe.

Tap-tap-tap on the door.

Another tap-tap. Then the handle revolved.

Mel ventured tentatively in. 'Hello, anyone at home –' Her voice took on a dying fall as she registered the disorder.

Circumspectly, she ventured further in, stumbling over a discarded black and white shoe.

Lying on the bed was the briefcase the passenger Grenville had dumped in his frustration at being recognised by the elderly Mister Kimber. Only now the briefcase was savagely ripped asunder and its contents ransacked.

. . . a soft footfall from the bathroom . . .

Stifling a scream, Mel grabbed the heavy shoe ready to defend herself as the divider slid open – a towheaded figure filled the gap.

'Phew! You might've warned me you were in there!'

'You're not supposed to be in here, Mel.'

'What about you? Going for a stroll! You just said that to put me off!' The brown eyes glinted with indignation.

'Why risk sticking two heads into the noose?' The Doctor's response was automatic. He had wandered to the dressing table where a handful of silver seeds lay scattered.

'Ever heard of safety in numbers?'

'Hmmmm. Never thought of that.' Intrigued, he was scooping the seeds into his palm.

Mel's concern was still with the chaos in the cabin. 'Looks as though someone's been in a fight for their life.'

'The question is, Mel, did they succeed?'

Cabin Six was not the only place in chaotic disarray. The *Hyperion*'s waste disposal unit was too.

A crumpled, uniformed attendant was spread-eagled on the floor where he had been left after an attack. Beyond him, a wheeled laundry bin had a sheet trailing over its side. Further on, closer to the massive steel iris shutter of the waste disposal unit, where warning lights were blinking furiously, was a single black and white shoe. Coming from beyond the shutter was the scrunching, churning chunter of the grinding blades.

To dispense with waste while in flight, all debris was fed into the powerful machine, pulverised, then evacuated into space . . . To all intents and purposes, the owner of the shoe had been given the same treatment . . .

Clutching his head, the attendant roused himself. Still confused, he instinctively followed the accepted drill and crawled towards the alarm.

The klaxon's wail penetrated even to the bridge, almost drowning the bleeping of the Commodore's intercom.

'Yes?' he growled into the intercom.

'Would you come down, sir?' Rudge's voice.

'Where?' Monosyllabic exasperation.

'Waste disposal unit. There's been an – er – accident.'

'Accident? Can't you deal with it?'

The wheedling tones again. 'I think you should be here, sir.'

Curtly, the Commodore flicked off the intercom. 'What I've done to be landed with him, I fail to comprehend!' Rising, he snatched up his white, peaked cap adorned with the gold braid of rank. 'Take over!' he rapped to the Duty Officer, and strode from the bridge.

The klaxon's frantic howling penetrated to Cabin Six too. The Doctor poked his head out into the corridor.

'What is it?' he yelled to Janet as she trotted past.

'Emergency in the waste disposal unit,' she replied, anxious to get to the lounge and reassure the passengers.

The Commodore's rugged face was suffused with anger.

'Accident! Why can't you use plain language,

37

Mister!' He addressed a chastened Rudge. 'Whoever's been dumped in there has been pulverised into fragments and sent floating into space! In my book that's murder!'

The Commodore was in little doubt that that was what had happened: the knocked-out attendant; the sheet trailing from the wastebin; the discarded shoe lying adjacent to the shutter; all led to this macabre verdict.

'Tell them to cut the klaxon,' he shouted to a guard as he crossed to the injured attendant. 'Have you called a Medic for this man?'

'Of course, sir. Straight away,' Rudge replied haughtily.

It had no effect on the Commodore. 'Then I suggest you begin earning your salary! Find out who that belongs to!' He was referring to the shoe.

'I may be able to help you there.' It was not the Security Officer's voice but the Doctor's. Unnoticed, he and Mel had arrived.

'Somehow that doesn't surprise me.' Sarcasm fitted the Commodore's mood.

'Perhaps I should leave it to the Security Officer,' challenged the Doctor.

Mel stepped into the breach. 'The passenger in Cabin Six sent for the Doctor. When we got there, he was gone.'

'It doesn't follow he wound up in the pulveriser.' Mel's contribution did nothing to mellow the Commodore's temper.

'The room was a wreck,' the Doctor volunteered.

'And there was a single shoe exactly the same pattern as that.' Mel indicated the discarded shoe.

'To be complete, the syllogism requires only the grim conclusion . . .' The Doctor gestured towards the pulveriser.

The Commodore was scathing. 'And naturally you've never met the man or know why he sent for you!'

'We don't even know his name.' That was true. When Mel received the message, no name was given: just the request for the Doctor to go to Cabin Six.

Rudge had been a bystander for long enough. 'It was Grenville, sir. A mineralogist.'

This did little to enlighten his commanding officer. 'Doctor, any suggestion why a mineralogist who wanted to see you should be killed?'

'None at all.'

'Or why it is whenever you appear on the scene people begin to die?' Spoken in anger and frustration by the Commodore, nevertheless the point seemed to subdue the Time Lord.

Not Mel. 'Hey! I don't care who you are, you've no right to say that to the Doctor!'

The Doctor shook his blonde, curly head. 'He has, Mel,' he said ruefully. 'He has every right. It's true . . .'

Quelling the klaxon had not allayed Sarah Lasky's and Doland's anxieties. They rose to greet Bruchner who came breathlessly into the lounge.

'Well?' demanded Lasky.

Before responding, he glanced nervously at the Mogarians seated at a nearby table.

'Never mind them,' snapped the Professor. Then, contradicting her own assertion, she clutched her subordinate's arm and hauled him to the far side of the lounge. Doland followed discreetly.

'Is the isolation room safe?'

'Yes. I had a word with the stewardess. She said the emergency was in the waste disposal unit.'

Lasky was visibly relieved. 'Then we can relax. Nothing to do with us.'

Bruchner's dark eyes burned with suppressed fury.

'That's your assessment, is it, Professor? The danger's past?'

The cryptic remark perplexed Doland: if all was well in the isolation room, then surely the danger *was* past.

What danger?

And what – or who – was in the isolation room?

These were the questions the Doctor would have posed had he been party to the exchange.

But he, uncharacteristically, was not asking questions at all . . .

6

The Booby Trap

'That's it then. End of the line.' Could this really be the Doctor talking?

It was. Sauntering into the gym, he paused at the sunlamp. 'Operates on vionesium. A speck no larger than a grain of sand will emit sunlight for umpteen years.'

'What d'you mean – end of the line?' Mel was nonplussed by this improbable behaviour.

Strangely dispirited, the Doctor ambled to the stationary walking machine. 'Our contact. Obviously it's he who's been pulverised.'

'So we give up?'

'What else?' He stepped onto the machine, and began walking on its moving platform.

'That hydroponic centre. I told you about the sudden panic when I was in there.' Mel was referring to the encounter between Lasky and Doland.

The Doctor showed no interest whatsoever.

But someone else did. Someone who was in the observation cubicle. Listening to every word being said . . .

'Immaterial and irrelevant.'

'I beg your pardon!'

Without interrupting his static walking, the Doctor delivered his homily. 'My dear Melanie, if you wish to pursue this completely arbitrary course, pray hurry along to the hydroponic centre. And leave me to my peregrinations . . .'

      ★   ★   ★

'Hold it! Hold it!' The Doctor flipped off the Matrix in the trial room, causing the screen to go black. The Inquisitor, Valeyard and Time Lords swivelled to face him. 'That wasn't as I remember it,' he asserted.

'How could you remember?' queried the Inquisitor. These events are in the Earth year 2986.'

'But I reviewed this section earlier . . .' The Doctor left the sentence unfinished. Disconcerted by what he had just seen, he could not get his thoughts together.

'In preparing your defence?' the Inquisitor prompted.

'Yes, but there have been changes. That isn't what happened. The girl – Mel – her information was important. I wouldn't have ignored it. Completely uncharacteristic. Even the words – misused – they didn't sound like mine.'

The Valeyard had heard enough. 'What isn't uncharacteristic is this resort to excuses and subterfuge.'

'Elaborate, Valeyard,' insisted the Inquisitor. 'Such accusations cannot be allowed to go unchallenged in *my* Court.'

'Apologies, my Lady.' The Valeyard's ingratiating tones barely accorded with his smug confidence. 'To gloss over the wilful death of Peri, the Doctor conveniently presents us with another companion.'

'Hardly a convenience. This is in the Doctor's future. He would not have met the young woman yet.'

The Valeyard bowed his elegant head. 'I stand corrected. But my assumption of why he has elected to pursue such an arbitrary course in aborting this tale still remains.'

'Arbitrary course . . .' repeated the Doctor to himself. 'Same words . . . an echo . . .' They were the very words he himself had used to Mel in the gymnasium.

'Your assumption, Valeyard?' The Inquisitor persevered with her interrogation of the gloating prosecutor.

A dramatic pause . . . then the *coup de grâce*: 'That she, too, is going to her death!'

'No! No!' The Doctor's alarm betrayed that this was what he feared. 'My Lady, I can't explain . . . I've . . . I've a feeling I'm being manipulated. The evidence is being distorted.'

'Preposterous! Absolutely preposterous!' The Valeyard was contemptuous. 'Forgive me, Sagacity . . . The idea the Matrix could lie. No, it is we who are being manipulated – to obscure the damaging truth.'

'Lies! Lies! This is complete fabrication!'

'The truth, Doctor,' persisted Valeyard. '*You* sent your companion down to the cargo hold. Into a situation which you described, I quote' – a brief glance at his notes – ' "Can't you sense it, Mel? Evil. There's evil in this place . . .!" '

'This is all wrong!' The Doctor was desperate now. 'Every instinct of which I'm capable would have compelled me to stop her!'

'Yet you did not . . .' The Valeyard emphasised each syllable.

No response from the dismayed Doctor.

The Inquisitor took over. 'Doctor, either you continue with your submission, or I must consider the evidence for the defence to be concluded.'

An air of expectancy gripped the Court: the elderly Time Lords in their russet robes; the Inquisitor, her classical looks enhanced by the white and gold filigree head-dress; the Valeyard with the inky black, tight-fitting skull cap outlining his pale regular features – all awaited the decision of the cornered prisoner.

The Doctor activated the Matrix.

*   *   *

Following her hunch, Mel slipped stealthily into the cargo hold. On tenterhooks, she skirted the main aisle, keeping to the perimeter of each pool of light to avoid detection. Every creak, every step tested her resolution as she made for the mellowly-lit hydroponic centre.

Passing a door marked *TECHNICAL STORES*, she froze.

'What are you doing prowling around down here?'

It was Edwardes, the young Communications Officer. He had come to the stores for a micro-component.

'Prowling? Why should I be prowling?' Mel had decided to bluff it out.

'Because this area is off-limits. And I suspect you know it.' The disapproval lacked conviction. Mel's vivacious and attractive personality had registered with the young officer when he had championed her on the bridge.

Exploiting his admiration, Mel eschewed subtlety. 'I wanted to have a peep at the hydroponic centre.'

'Any reason in particular?'

'I think it could tie in with the mysterious Mayday call that was sent from your communications room to the TARDIS.'

Edwardes rubbed his neck as he remembered the unpleasant sensation of being knocked cold by an unseen assailant.

'I'm not going to touch anything,' she promised. 'What harm could it do?' Edwardes' obduracy was melting as he gazed into the beguiling brown eyes with their long-fringed lashes.

'I'll probably regret this. But come on: a conducted tour only. No wandering off on your own.'

Little did he realise how prophetic that prediction would be as he led Mel towards the hydroponic centre.

Mel used the occasion for more prying. 'Tell me, who is that woman with the dragon's voice?'

'Professor Sarah Lasky. She's an agronomist. So are her two assistants, Bruchner and Doland.'

If they were agronomists, Mel knew the study of plant life was their subject and therefore this specially lit and watered centre must have been set up for them.

Edwardes confirmed this. 'Yes, we had to allocate part of the hold.'

They had reached the outer gate and while Edwardes pressed his palm against the PPR lock, Mel read the warning notice. 'Why is only low spectrum light allowed in the place?'

'Something to do with photosynthesis. Low spectrum light allows the plants to stay dormant.'

The outer gate swung open. 'I'll go ahead,' he said. 'Don't want you breaking your pretty neck in the dark.' He placed his hand on the inner mesh gate.

'*Aaaaah!*'

In a cascade of sparks, Edwardes was slammed against the fence. Lights flared. His body convulsed. A powerful current surged through his quivering frame, crucifying him. Arms outstretched, his electrified corpse slumped to the floor. A high-tension cable had been malevolently attached to the mesh, creating a death trap.

Aghast, Mel instinctively backed several paces, unable to take in the horror. Shaken free by the impact, the cable was arcing, bathing Edwardes' body in intermittent flashes of white light.

Screaming, Mel fled from the hold to fetch help.

But, not only Edwardes' dead body was being bathed in the white light . . . the arcing from the cable reached beyond him to the giant pods.

The nearest pod began to rupture . . . a small slit severed its central seam.

The same with the next pod.

And the next.

45

Right along the row, the pods started to burst.

Eerie enough in itself.

But from the first ruptured seam came an even more horrendous sight: a flexing, waxy, olive, leaf-veined hand clawed through the ever widening gap . . .

7

A Fateful Harvest

Hair streaming, in a turmoil of terror, Mel streaked blindly through the dark cargo hold and blundered into two patrolling guards who had been alerted by her screams.

'What are you doing here? You were told –'

'Back there!' cried Mel. 'Edwardes! He's dead!' She gestured towards the hydroponic centre.

So evident was her distress that the second guard, without waiting for instruction, ran to investigate.

'He just touched the fence and –'

'Save your explanation for the Commodore, lady.' The first guard was less responsive. He played by the book.

A sensible maxim as it was to prove.

'Have you found him?' he called to his colleague.

'Yes. He's dead all right,' came the grim response.

'Stay with him. I'll send help.' Fierce with rage over the slaughter of his comrade, Mel's captor bundled her roughly from the hold. For once she did not argue.

The still arcing light cast the bent figure of the remaining guard into silhouette as he knelt beside the body of the Communications Officer.

It also illuminated the giant pods . . . and the waxy, leaf-veined, claw-like hands groping through the rupturing shucks . . .

But there was more.

A shuck, split wide open, was empty . . .

Whatever had been inside was now free . . .

Free and shuffling towards the unsuspecting guard. . . .

*　　*　　*

'Another death, Doctor?' pronounced the Valeyard to the assembled judges in the Trial Room. 'But for the caprice of chance, the victim would have been the woman, Mel. Your culpability is beyond question.'

The Inquisitor was inclined to concur. 'You could have prevented her from venturing into the cargo hold. Instead you appeared to encourage her.'

Indignation furrowed the Doctor's pleasant features. 'When I reviewed the Matrix, that isn't what happened! There's something out of sync!' He knew this to be true but could not understand how that could be. After all, the Matrix was inviolable. Or so he had always believed.

'More futile grasping at straws. When the facts tell against you, cry fraud!' The Valeyard's insinuation carried weight. The Time Lords nodded in agreement.

'Do you wish to reconsider, Doctor?' asked the Inquisitor.

'No. I'm being manipulated. But the only means of discovering why and by whom, is to press on!'

*　　*　　*

Against the infinite velvet blackness of space, the titanic, multi-decked *Hyperion III* glided implacably onwards.

Nothing untoward hindered its flight.

Inside its vast, futuristic interior, a different scenario was unfolding. Especially in the cargo hold.

A grille from an airduct had been removed.

Legs protuding, Edwardes' body was being tortuously hauled into the exposed duct.

By whom? Or by what?

The only clue was a waxy, olive, leaf-veined, clawing hand yanking Edwardes' remains from view . . .

Then it reached for the corpse of the second guard . . .

'Why aren't you wearing a pulsometer?'

Unknown to the apathetic Doctor, Professor Lasky had entered the gymnasium. She waggled a pulsometer under his nose. 'The heart should be monitored while exercising.'

The Doctor halted the walking machine. '*Which* heart would you suggest, Madam?' He squinted at the meter. Clipped to the ear, it would register the heart-beats of the wearer. Time Lords have two hearts, but Lasky wouldn't be aware of this. The Doctor decided to play the fool with this domineering pedagogue. 'Unfortunately it doesn't register a double pulse.'

'Double pulse? What are you? A comedian?'

'More of a clown, actually. Care to hear my rendering of *On With The Motley*?'

Lasky was spared this excruciating experience by the arrival of Rudge. 'Excuse me, Professor Lasky.' He spoke politely to her, not so to the Time Lord. 'Doctor, you're required on the bridge!'

'The Commodore wants a chat? Good, I shall enjoy that.'

'I don't think you'll find enjoyment's on the agenda!'

Beyond the neat array of sophisticated controls, through the navigational window, the serene panorama of space was at odds with the tenseness gripping the inquest on the bridge.

With the guard who had marched her from the fatal scene in the cargo hold at her side, Mel stood before the stern-faced Commodore.

'I don't need anyone to defend me!' She was not easily cowed. 'I'm quite capable of defending myself!'

Ignoring her defiance, the Commodore addressed the Doctor. 'How long have you known this woman?'

Unaware of what had taken place, the Doctor prevaricated. 'Time is a comparative concept, Commodore.'

'Not now, Doctor!' Mel was haunted by the sight of Edwardes' electrocution on the mesh fence. 'Just answer the question!'

'I should accept the advice and drop the sophistry. Can you vouch for her?' This was the Commodore.

'Completely. Utterly. What's this all about, Mel?'

'The Communications Officer's dead and they think I did it!'

'She was caught running from the scene. She can't deny that,' Rudge accused.

'I haven't tried!' protested Mel. 'I persuaded Edwardes to show me the hydroponic centre. It was booby-trapped.'

'Booby-trapped?' repeated the Doctor.

'Yes. If it hadn't been for Edwardes it would've been me who was killed.'

During this exchange, the intercom had buzzed.

'*What!*' exploded Rudge into the instrument. 'Are you certain?'

'What is it?'

'Medical team report, sir. They went to the hold to attend to Edwardes . . . and they say there's no sign of him anywhere.'

'But there must be,' said Mel.

'Maybe he wasn't dead,' the Doctor suggested gently. 'The weird atmosphere down there could lead to phantasmagoria.'

'Oh, come on! You know me. Am I prone to that sort

50

of imagination?' She wasn't. Mel was a skilled computer programmer back on Earth. Her talents were practical; her outlook on life sane and level-headed, without any of the flights of fancy to which the Doctor's eccentricities might be heir.

The Commodore rounded on Mel's escort. 'I thought you left a man down there!'

'I did, sir.'

'Rudge?'

'They say there's no sign of him either.'

'The guard's disappeared too?' Mel was puzzled but realised it established her innocence. 'Now, perhaps you'll accept I'm not responsible. You've had me in custody!'

'The perfect alibi, Commodore,' ventured the Doctor.

'Organise a search, Mister Rudge.' The Commodore was terse. 'I want those two men found!'

Obediently, guards at his heels, Rudge departed. The Commodore glowered at the Doctor. 'Since you put in an appearance, first a passenger was fed into the pulveriser and now my Communications Officer and a guard have gone missing! Two, if not all three, killed. Murdered.'

Mel shuddered and hugged herself at the gruesome images the recital prompted.

The Commodore was not finished. 'But you – standing there in a divine state of innocence – you can't tell me what's happening on my ship, can you!'

Meeting the challenge full on, Mel gave him a reply. 'I can. The answer's simple enough. You've got a killer on board!'

8

The Demeter Seeds

Crr-a-a-s-ssh!

The shattering of fragmenting china startled the sentry. It came from inside the isolation room.

Indecisively, he leaned closer.

Listened.

He had no idea what was beyond that door. Nor did he dare try to find out. Orders were unequivocal: protect but do not enter.

Doland emerged from the isolation room carrying a tray cluttered with broken crockery. Food stains soiled his white smock. 'An accident. No cause for concern.' He dumped the tray beside the door. 'The stewardess will collect that.'

As Doland left, the sentry gazed disgustedly at the debris on the tray.

Unconsciously he rested his hand on his phaser holster. An apprehension which had not abated when Janet arrived. But before either could comment, Rudge came strolling along the corridor.

He was in the high dudgeon of the weak in temperament: the search for the missing crew members had drawn a blank. A grimace at the mess on the tray. 'Again?'

Janet nodded. 'What's going on in there?'

'Don't ask me! I'm only the Security Officer!'

The statement served to fuel the sentry's unease.

Nor did time lessen the tension.

Passing on his way to the lounge, the Doctor waved a

breezy greeting. The sentry's response was to tighten his grip on the phaser.

Mel failed to register this byplay. She was in mid-lecture. 'Look, you can't just adopt a passive role.' The Doctor was, to all appearances, still remaining obstinately in the neutral corner. 'We were sent for, remember?'

'I'm cogitating.'

'About what?'

The Doctor indicated the sentry by the door to the isolation room. 'Whether that guard's job is to keep unwanted visitors out, or . . .'

'Keep someone in?'

'Intriguing, isn't it?'

'Does seem strange, I admit, an armed guard outside an isolation room.'

Their voices died away. Alone again, the sentry listened at the door.

Silence. . . .

There was silence, too, in the cargo hold. An almost eerie silence. Just the muffled throb of the engines. No sign of the two bodies. The grill of the airduct was back in place.

Enzu, the Mogarian with the sash, came stealthily in. His protective suit and opaque goggles reflected the dim auxiliary lighting as he padded furtively between the packing crates.

Reaching the hydroponic centre, Enzu glanced briefly at the disconnected cable before crossing to the pods.

His goggles were slowly scanning the giant empty shucks, when something captured his attention: caught on the edge of the air duct, trapped by the grille, was a wisp of waxy, olive-green leaf . . .

He plucked it free and felt its texture with his gloved

hand . . . then he pressed his helmeted head against the grille. A distant, vaguely alien, murmuring could be heard . . .

Further investigation was aborted by a more immediate crisis. The imminent approach of Doland and Bruchner threatened to expose the Mogarian's trespassing. Swiftly he sought cover in the cargo hold.

Bruchner's thin face was flushed with anger. 'No matter how you and Professor Lasky rationalise the situation, we should not have proceeded to the point we've reached.'

'Why you became a scientist, Bruchner, baffles me,' replied Doland. 'You have the temperament of an over-cautious rabbit.'

The debate intrigued Enzu. Moving quietly, he kept them within earshot.

'Did you leave the gates open?' The gaping gates alarmed Doland.

Already in an acute state of anxiety, the volatile Bruchner made straight for the pods. 'Doland! The pods! Every one of them! Empty!'

Doland hurriedly joined him. 'Some fool must have introduced light into the centre.'

'Introduced light!' Bruchner's self control was in danger of crumbling. 'We're confronted with a catastrophe and that's your reaction! *Don't you realise what's been unleashed!*'

How different events would have proved had the Doctor overheard this conversation. As it was, he and Mel, knowing nothing of the impending disaster, were entering the lounge.

Turning to the Doctor, she extended her hand. 'Where are they?'

'Where are who?'

'You know exactly what I mean. Where are those

seeds? The ones you picked up in the wrecked cabin. Or did you think I'd forgotten?'

The Doctor rummaged in his pocket and extracted the Demeter seeds. Mel tried to take a couple.

'Why d'you want them?' He closed his fist.

Mel indicated Professor Lasky who was seated at the far end of the lounge reading a detective novel. 'She's an agronomist. I'm going to ask her about the seeds.'

'Is she? Agronomist? Hmmm. Better leave me to cope with her.'

'*You?*'

'It requires tact and finesse. I'm blessed with both.'

En route to Lasky, he smiled benignly at the Mogarians who were absorbed in an electronic board game. There were only the two of them, Atza and Ortezo: Enzu, of course, was in the cargo hold.

'Professor Lasky.'

She glanced up as the Doctor spoke. Not too happy at being disturbed, she was even less pleased on recognising the Time Lord. 'Oh, it's you, the comedian. What d'you want?'

Her aggressive reception did not deter him. 'I understand you're an agronomist.'

'Thremmatologist, to be precise.'

'A thremmatologist.' He held out the seeds. 'Then you're well qualified to tell me about –'

'Stewardess!' Lasky's strident roar brought Janet scurrying. 'Stewardess!'

'Something wrong, Professor?'

'Fetch the Security Officer!'

'Can I help?'

'At once!'

Janet clicked on her communicator. 'Mister Rudge to the passenger lounge, please.' Trying to maintain her air of calm, she returned to her questioning. 'May I be told what's wrong, Professor?'

Lasky's reply was raucous and adamant. She levelled an accusing finger at the Doctor.

'This man's a thief!'

The Time Lord was lost for words.

Not Mel.

Looking at his bewildered face, she shook her head. 'Tact? Finesse? Now what have you landed us in!'

9

A Change of Course

If the Doctor was courting trouble, so, too, was Enzu. Dodging between islands of crates in his advance on the work hut, his fleeting shadow was spotted by Bruchner.

'What was that?' On edge, nerves taut, Bruchner squinted into the gloomy cargo section.

'Nothing. Pull yourself together, Bruchner.'

'There's someone in the hold.'

Doland was not convinced but to pacify his colleague he peered about. 'You're allowing hysteria to –'

'I know what I saw! There was a movement!' Bruchner started in the direction of the hold. Doland tagged along.

In full retreat, Enzu was compelled to dart across the main aisle to reach the exit.

Glimpsing an indistinct figure, the two scientists hurried to intercept.

Too late. The Mogarian had escaped.

If either man had recognised the intruder, he was not saying. Doland gave a fatalistic shrug and Bruchner's doom-laden eyes had already returned to the hydroponic centre and the empty pods.

A change of mood had overcome their leader, Professor Lasky.

'That puts an entirely different complexion on the issue,' she declared to Mel. A friendly smile embellished her face, heightening her mature but extremely attractive features.

Mel had intervened to explain how the Doctor had acquired the seeds. She – and only she – was the recipient of the Professor's benefaction.

'A pity your friend the comedian wasn't as lucid!'

The Doctor's protest came quickly. 'I never got a chance –'

'Although I can't understand what they were doing in Cabin Six,' said Lasky over him. 'Or why a mineralogist would steal them.'

'Are they special, Professor?' asked Mel.

'Just what I was about –'

'The Demeter seeds? Yes, they are.' Again Lasky cut the Doctor off. 'They represent a tremendous advance. A colossal leap.'

'Do they? How –?'

'What did you call them? The Demeter seeds?' Even Mel was now interrupting the Doctor. It seemed the two women were completely ignoring his presence. An unusual and not enjoyable experience for the extrovert Time Lord. He tried answering a question since he had failed to ask one. 'Name of a god –'

'Food of the gods.' Lasky had done it again! 'Bruchner, my assistant – bit of a romantic, highly strung – he christened them.'

Rudge, tardily responding to the intercom summons, had arrived with a guard. Janet, anticipating his arrival, was waiting by the entrance to explain.

The Doctor had not given up. 'That still doesn't –'

'He wasn't just being pretentious.' Nor had Lasky given up. 'They'll increase yields threefold. And, more, they'll grow in desert sands.'

By now, Rudge, officiously marching across the lounge, had reached the professor's side.

'What is it, man? Don't stand there hovering!' she barked at Rudge.

'You sent for him!' The Doctor actually managed to

58

finish a sentence.

'I did?' Incredulity, then recall. 'Oh, yes. Not to worry.'

'But I do worry,' came Rudge's bland reply. 'Especially when serious allegations are made. You accused the Doctor of being a thief.'

'Oh that? A mistake. The fellow may be a fool but he's not a criminal.'

Brows drawn, blue eyes glaring in resentment at the purveyor of the back-handed compliment, the Doctor absently tossed a Demeter seed into his mouth and chewed indignantly!

The shenanigans in the lounge would have been dismissed as trivial by the Commodore. Apparent murder and disappearing bodies were uppermost on his list of priorities.

His dark, intelligent eyes were studying the concave window above the control console on the bridge where near-space showed against a navigational grid.

'Project our course through the sector ahead.'

The duty officer coded in the request. A curving line bisected the grid and a series of figures flashed up on the display panel.

'Put us onto a straighter course. Reduce the diversion to a point-nought-three safety margin.'

The duty officer obeyed, then read the responding dials. 'I estimate that brings our ETA forward by seventy-two hours, sir.'

'Seventy-two hours closer to getting expert investigators aboard.' He rose. 'Do it!' Commodore Travers was a man whose command brooked no discussion. His subordinate began making the adjustments.

Against a background where spiral galaxies and nebula

clusters predominated, the *Hyperion III*'s boosters emitted staccato bursts, shifting the massive vehicle's trajectory.

The sound of the rocket boosters could be heard in the lounge. Although not intrusive, the noise created a constrained stir. Atza and Ortezo gripped the arms of their chairs and the Commodore, descending the twisting staircase, caught the elderly Mister Kimber as he almost lost balance.

'There is no need for concern.' His authoritative voice caused all to look his way. Even Lasky, sitting at a table with the Doctor and Mel, glanced up from her book.

'A navigational adjustment. As you can see, it doesn't even require my presence on the bridge.' His smile was completely reassuring. 'For your information, the change of course will bring our landfall forward by seventy-two hours.'

The Mogarian Atza plucked at the Commodore's sleeve. An unintelligible guttural dialogue was emitted from his electronic box.

'Switch on your translator,' advised the Commodore.

Atza rapped the stud and the red light gleamed on his electronic box. 'Surely we are approaching the sector with the Black Hole of Tartarus.'

'That's correct.'

Ortezo switched on his translator as Atza pursued his query. 'If you are saving time, we must be going closer to the Black Hole.'

Enzu entered and joined his fellow Mogarians.

'There is no danger. The safety margin is more than adequate.' Never his strong suit, the Commodore's diplomacy was wearing thin.

Only the Doctor was blatantly listening to the brittle exchange. Both Janet and Rudge concealed their interest; the stewardess by distributing refreshments, the

Security Officer by concentrating on a duty roster.

Arriving and quickly summing up the situation, Doland stayed the agitated Bruchner by accepting two beakers of coffee from Janet.

'That is hardly a denial, Commodore,' Ortezo contributed, his light blinking.

'Simply a bromide,' added Enzu.

'You've sought reassurance. I've given it.' The Commodore, unused to having his decisions questioned, was making a deliberate effort to remain polite.

'That word "reassurance" bears sinister undertones for we Mogarians,' said Ortezo.

'Indeed?' The Commodore was curt.

'It is the word the Earthlings used when first they persuaded us to allow them to sink mines on Mogar,' Ortezo continued.

'A limited concession was all they requested.' Atza was by far the most aggressive of the three. 'Now they are stripping our planet bare.'

The Commodore made no reply.

'Truth is a stranger to the Earthlings,' stated Enzu.

The Commodore had had enough. 'If you'll excuse me. Politics do not come into my realm of influence.'

'Then they should.' The Doctor's interference simply accelerated the Commodore's departure. It did little to modify the sentiments of the Mogarians either.

'Who are you? Another prospector?'

'Only of knowledge. I've visited your planet. It's very rich in natural resources.'

The Doctor's kindly manner did not have the desired effect. Ortezo's rejoinder was forceful. 'Which will soon be exhausted if these Earthlings are not restrained. They are going through the Universe like a plague of interplantary locusts!'

*　　*　　*

61

'Are we to be subjected to a dissertation on inter-planetary politics now, Sagacity?' The Valeyard was on his feet.

The Doctor rounded on him angrily. 'Is that all you think it was!'

'Mining rights. Mogarians versus Earthlings. What else would you call that?'

'You're so pathetically intent on incriminating me that you're not watching what's going on!'

'My eyes never left the Matrix screen.'

'You may have been selected to prosecute me, Vale-yard, but I pray you'll never be chosen to defend me!'

'An occasion that will not arise, Doctor. Your lives are forfeit as I have ably proven.'

'Enough!' The Inquisitor would countenance no further argument. 'Is this case to be resolved in a battle of words? Or to be conducted via the Matrix?'

'Something vital happened in that scene and the Valeyard perversely directed his attention to more mundane matters.'

'Then for pity's sake tell us what it was and enjoy your moment of triumph,' urged the Valeyard.

The Doctor's tone moderated as he replied. 'Triumph? There is no cause for celebration. One of the occupants in that lounge is about to die.'

'Another murder?' The prospect had no daunting influence on the Valeyard.

'Yes. And if you'd been watching, you would know the intended victim.'

True. The clue had been clearly signposted.

The Doctor switched on the Matrix screen. 'You'll not have long to wait . . .'

10

Death Of An Impostor

Intergalactic law decreed that the Commodore was absolute master of the *Hyperion III* and everyone aboard her. Sipping a beaker of coffee which Rudge had just collected, Commodore Travers felt anything but in control.

He cast a jaundiced eye over the lounge. Mister Kimber was dozing in a recliner. The trio of self-absorbed scientists, near the drinks dispenser, were in deep, hushed discussion. Janet was circulating solicitously between tables, and close to the three Mogarians, engrossed in a hologram game, was the pair for whom the Commodore's feelings were ambivalent, to say the least – the Doctor and Mel.

'You've drawn a blank where Edwardes is concerned?'

'Yes, sir,' Rudge replied. 'Perhaps if we searched the passenger cabins.'

'No. The passengers are already uneasy. D'you want them to realise they're trapped with a killer on the loose?' He was in no doubt that was the position. How else could Edwardes have been electrocuted? How else could his body and the guard have disappeared without trace? How else could a passenger have been tipped into the pulveriser?

Brilliant purple imbued the hologram, signalling victory. Courteously the two defeated contestants nodded in graceful acceptance, then all three Mogarians fixed tubes to their helmets through which to suck their cooling coffee.

The Doctor's idle gaze transferred from them to his companion. 'You've been very quiet, Mel. Not quite your style to go into a brown study.'

'Brown study?' Mel teased. 'Is the vocabulary of all the Time Lords so antediluvian –'

Enzu began retching and choking!

He clutched at the neck band of his suit . . . collapsed from his seat to the floor, convulsing . . . spine arching!

In reflex action, the Doctor reached him first. The tremors racking Enzu subsided as the Doctor fumbled to unclip his helmet.

'Are you trying to kill him!' The Commodore swiped the Doctor's hands away from the helmet.

'I'm trying to save him!'

'He will die if you remove his helmet!' screamed Atza, his translator light blinking.

'Mogarians can't breathe our air. Surely you're aware of that!' boomed Rudge.

'*He's not a Mogarian!*'

The Doctor's baffling statement struck everyone speechless.

Except Mel. 'He's not?'

'Then who is he?' The others may have dismissed the Doctor's declaration as fanciful, but the Commodore knew the Time Lord too well for that.

'If you'll permit me to remove the helmet, we'll discover the answer.' He resumed the task. 'Though I fear the poor fellow is beyond help.'

Even the voluble Lasky was mute while the helmet was eased clear. The bearded face revealed was that of the missing passenger: the man who occupied Cabin Six; whose room was ransacked and whose shoe was found beside the pulveriser.

Janet identified him. 'Mister Grenville!'

'Grenville?' The Doctor was puzzled.

'The passenger from Cabin Six who's supposed to have been dumped in the pulveriser!' The Commodore's bitter explanation brought a bizarre response from the Doctor.

'His name isn't Grenville. It's Hallet!'

11

A Plethora of Suspects

Supervised by the Commodore, a stretcher party had borne the latest murder victim from the lounge.

'Poor Mister Hallet.' The elderly Kimber was white with shock. 'I knew it was Hallet. I recognised him, remember?'

His question was directed at Janet, who shook her head. In fact, they had all heard the greeting, including the two Mogarians and the three scientists.

'But he denied it. Insisted his name was Grenville.' Rudge seemed more affronted than puzzled.

'He would . . .' The Doctor's interjection did nothing to clarify the situation. He studied the others: which of them had murdered Hallet?

Mel's thoughts were more immediate. 'Well, whatever he's called, Grenville or Hallet, why did he stage his own death in the pulveriser?'

'This gentleman's given us the answer.'

Mister Kimber was astounded to see the Doctor was indicating him. 'I have?'

'Hallet presumably had been assigned to investigate something – or somebody – on this ship. Then he had the bad luck to be recognised. A chance encounter that put his mission in jeopardy.'

'Are you saying we had an undercover agent aboard and I wasn't informed?' The Security Officer's pomposity would have been comic on a less sad occasion.

'You may have been a suspect.'

'Me!'

'And everyone else on the journey.' The Doctor's conclusion encompassed the assembled listeners.

'Is this guesswork? Or have you got more tricks up your sleeve?'

'No tricks, Mister Rudge. I knew Hallet. And admired him. But I assure you, until I removed that helmet, I had no idea he was aboard.'

'All nice and lily white, Doctor. But it still leaves a nasty little problem.'

'It does?'

'How did you know the dead man wasn't a Mogarian?'

*　　*　　*

'Yes, how did you know?' The Valeyard rasped for the benefit of the whole Trial Room. 'Have you been editing the Matrix and denying the Court evidence to which it is entitled?'

'That would be a serious offence if true, Doctor.'

'At the risk of being impertinent, my Lady, I must point out that you, the Valeyard and every Time Lord in this Court could have acquired similar knowledge.'

The Inquisitor's regal head inclined towards the prisoner's dock. 'Perhaps we may hear your explanation.'

'With respect, you will not hear it from me.' He pressed the button on the Matrix, causing the images on the screen to rewind rapidly to the scene in the lounge when Atza plucked at the Commodore's sleeve and began to speak in an unintelligible, guttural voice.

'Switch on your translator.' Atza switches on and a red light flickers on his translator box. 'Surely we are approaching the sector with the Black Hole of Tartarus.'

The Doctor fast-forwarded the reprise to Enzu's entrance, cutting in on the Commodore's speech.

'*There's no danger. The safety margin is more than adequate.*'

'*That is hardly a denial,*' says Ortezo, *the light flickering on his translator box.*

'*Simply a bromide,*' adds Enzu . . . *but no light winked on his translator box.* . . .

With a flourish, the Doctor stopped the Matrix. 'As you saw, the bogus Mogarian did not switch on his translator!'

'Very astute of you, Doctor,' conceded the Valeyard, sourly. 'But don't stop there. Let us assume the murdered man – Grenville or Hallet, what you will – was responsible for the Mayday call.' He paused for agreement. The Doctor did not respond. He wanted the Valeyard to continue before he was prepared to make any commitment.

'Perhaps you'll now direct your deductive gifts towards justifying his extraordinary behaviour.' He smirked, sure he had gained an advantage; especially as the Inquisitor was nodding approvingly.

'Yes. To rate it no higher, Doctor, the investigator Hallet's methods were unorthodox.'

'Agreed.' The Doctor beamed at her, obviously not feeling disadvantaged by the Valeyard's cunning. 'And I am indebted to the prosecutor for putting his finger on the nub of my defence. The reason why I could no longer stand on the sidelines.'

He activated the Matrix.

*　　*　　*

Against the most spectacular backdrop in the firmament – the Perseus Arm of the Milky Way – Mel and the Doctor gazed down. They stood on the balcony at the top of the spiral staircase, just below the transparent ceiling of the lounge.

'Anybody there could've poisoned his drink!' It had been verified that Enzu had died from poisoning.

'Providing us with a plethora of suspects,' agreed the Doctor.

'Us? Do I detect a commitment at last?'

He nodded.

'Because of Hallet's death? You said you admired him.'

'I did.' There was sorrow in the Doctor's tone. 'He was one of a rare breed. A maverick. Even the highly-organised society of the thirtieth century has a need for his kind. He'll be missed.'

While he was speaking, Bruchner, after consulting Lasky and Doland, quit the lounge.

The Doctor fumbled in his pocket and pulled out the silver Demeter seeds. 'Hallet left these deliberately for me to find . . .'

'To lead you to where I've been telling you all along. The hydroponic centre!'

Perhaps if the Doctor had heeded Mel earlier, many lives would have been saved.

Instead, another was in immediate peril of being lost.

Danger came from within the ventilation shafts which honeycombed the ship's interior: a network large enough in places for a man to walk upright . . . Only the beings now haunting the air ducts were not human . . . For them, the world was an alien habitat tinted in a sickly green haze.

One of these denizens, reconnoitring, had encountered an impasse. Its thorn-tipped talons shook a grille that gave access to the corridor near the isolating room.

Curious about the metallic clinking, the sentry hesitated in two minds about deserting his post to investigate. Inquisitiveness sent him on an assignation with death. He sauntered towards the grille –

'What are you doing away from your post!'

Bruchner's irate reprimand caused the sentry to beat a contrite retreat.

'The isolation room is under no circumstances to be left unguarded! If it happens again, I shall report you to the Commodore!'

Yanking on a surgical mask, he stomped into the isolation room.

Ironically the resentful sentry would never appreciate that the reprimand had forestalled his extermination . . .

The Doctor had, at last, conceded that Mel could be right about the hydroponic centre. Crossing the hold, they passed the TARDIS, reminding Mel again of Hallet.

'Hallet must've sent the Mayday call.'

'He wanted me here as a catalyst. To divert attention from his own activities.'

'You'd do that without being asked!' Her joking was a cover for reluctance as they neared the gate that had been the setting for Edwardes' death.

'Hallet was an unorthodox man, Mel, but he was also a subtle man. So why did he resort to blunderbuss tactics? Why did he use me as a Judas goat?'

'He was running out of time. The Mayday message said as much.' She began to quote the message that had appeared on their monitor in the TARDIS. ' "*perative traitor be identified before landing Earth*". I'd guess the incomplete word was "imperative", wouldn't you?' The memory of that convulsing, electrified body crowded in.

The Doctor, aware of Mel's thoughts, tried to divert her. 'I've always envied you that, Mel.'

70

'Envied me what?'

'The ability you've got for almost total recall.'

'Compliments! You *are* undergoing a change!'

'I could be comparing you with an elephant. Figuratively speaking,' he teased, looking fondly at the diminutive Mel whose waist measured a mere twenty-two inches and whose head barely reached to the level of his shoulders. 'They never forget.' An unfortunate metaphor that was only too true.

'Doctor . . . I realise you're trying to take my mind off . . . poor Edwardes.'

'If you'd rather wait here . . .'

Bracing herself, Mel preceded him through the gate.

Following her, the Doctor delved into his pocket, extracting a piece of waxy, olive green leaf. It was the leaf Enzu – or Hallet as he was now know to have been – had found attached to the air duct when he was exploring the hold.

'What've you got there?' asked Mel.

'Came from Hallet's pocket.'

He began darting about the hydroponic centre, trying to find a match for the leaf.

'I didn't see you take it.'

'Neither did anyone else. Another of my skills!'

Intrigued, he was prodding and poking the empty pods. 'What d'you make of these pods, Mel?'

'I'm not into agronomy. Ask the Professor.'

'Thremmatology. The Professor said she was a thremmatologist.' The texture of the shucks occupied him: a coarse, rubbery membrane.

'You're going to have to enlighten me. That's out of my range.'

'It's the science of breeding or propagating animals and plants under domestication.'

Measuring it for size, he stepped inside a pod. The Doctor was tall, but he could have been wearing the

71

busby of a Hussar and yet have height to spare.

'I'm not much wiser.'

'Think about it, Mel. You've got a good brain. Think.' He shuffled, positioning himself, sentry-fashion, in the pod. 'Wonder what came out of here?'

12

The Isolation Room

'Will you end this charade!'

The 'charade' was Lasky's slavish adherence to her punishing exercise routine. Clad in a pale blue tracksuit, she was hoisting spring-loaded weights in the well-equipped gym. To Bruchner it was a pathetic pretence of normality.

'You both know we're on the brink of disaster!' The chary Doland was the other recipient of his castigation.

'All I know is, you're panicking. There is nothing we can do!' In contrast with his associate, Doland spoke with his customary stoicism.

'You've no conscience, Doland. I'm aware of that. But you, Professor, I expected you to grasp the enormity of our folly.'

What folly?

Could he be referring to the secret of the isolation room?

Or was he referring to the bursting of the giant pods . . . and whatever had escaped from them?

'So you're suggesting we jeopardise years of scientific research for the sake of some hypothetical danger?' countered Doland.

'Exactly!' agreed Lasky. 'We've no reason to believe the results of our experiments are other than benign.'

'Benign!' Bruchner rubbed his balding pate. 'Have you been in the isolation room lately, Professor?'

'An unfortunate mishap that has no relevance to this situation. In any case, it's academic now.'

'I lack your lofty detachment!'

'Do you also lack loyalty, Bruchner? To your colleagues?' Lasky's anger was biting. 'Before we left Mogar, we agreed our discovery should be divulged to no-one – *no-one* – until we reached Earth. Unless you can produce concrete evidence to prove there is danger, I expect you to keep your word!'

Bruchner was not cowed. 'You simply don't understand, do you? The crime we're committing in the name of science will make us infamous!' He paused. 'Always assuming there's anyone left alive to pass judgment, that is!'

This harbinger of woe had a wider audience than just Lasky and Doland.

High up above the parallel bars, blurred by the grille of a vent, was an indistinct shape . . . The overwrought debate had been witnessed by one of the inhabitants that now infested the air ducts . . .

Not that this scourge was solely confined to the ventilation system. A removed grille in the bathroom of Cabin Ten was evidence that the menace was spreading . . .

'Have you decided to get some rest, sir?' Janet enquired of the octogenarian Kimber who, troubled by his part in Hallet's death, had abandoned the lounge to seek the privacy of his cabin.

'Yes,' he quavered. 'Though I doubt that I'll sleep. At my age, one doesn't want to be reminded of mortality.'

His gnarled fingers grasped the door knob of Cabin Ten.

'May I fetch you a warm drink?'

Gratitude lit his wrinkled features. 'Thank you, that's very gracious.'

Entering the cabin, Kimber unbuttoned his jacket

and hung it in the wardrobe, meticulously smoothing any creases. With the diligent precision of lifelong habit, he unbuckled his wristwatch and laid it fastidiously on the dressing table. Its double dial recorded the hour on Earth and on Mogar simultaneously, and was precious to the old man not for its intrinsic value but because it was a gift from the son he was going to visit. A tiny glow of pleasure ousted thoughts of the murder and he sought solace in memories of the past: in particular, a picnic on the Yorkshire Dales with his four grandchildren.

Uncuffing his shirt sleeves, he slid open the bathroom divider . . . and immediately recoiled in horror – a waxy, leaf-veined hand shot out and implanted a thorn in the aged man's scrawny neck.

Venom from the thorn callously strangled his stricken cry. The final picture Mister Kimber had of this life was most assuredly not of his native heath.

A tap-tap on the cabin door. 'It's the stewardess, sir. I've brought your warm drink.'

With scant regard for the respect usually accorded the dead, Kimber's body was dragged into the bathroom and the divider closed . . .

After knocking again, Janet ventured in, expecting to find the elderly passenger awaiting her.

He wasn't. He'd just turned on the shower. She could hear the gushing water. 'Shall I put it on the dressing table?' Not wanting the drink to get cold, she shouted loudly enough to be heard above the splattering spray.

'Shall I, sir?' she persisted.

A pause . . . 'Ye-e-esss,' came a sibilant reply.

But not from Mister Kimber's lips.

His lips never moved.

Tapping along beside the silent, musing Doctor, Mel

was taking two paces to his one. Used to these reveries, she resisted the temptation to offer him the proverbial 'penny' for them.

He was marshalling the questions he intended to put to the scientists about the pods. For, unless he was mistaken, they were central to the mystery.

'There's Lasky.' Mel had spotted the professor, mouth and nostrils muzzled by a surgical mask, exiting from the isolation room. A curt nod to the sentry and she departed in the opposite direction.

The Doctor, instead of pursuing his quarry, came to a precipitate halt.

'What's a thremmatologist been doing in an isolation room wearing a surgical mask?'

'As there's only one way to find out, you've got two problems,' replied the ever practical Mel.

'Two?'

'Apart from getting rid of the guard, you're going to need a mask. And you can hardly ask the Professor to lend you hers!'

'Hmmm.' The Doctor pondered the problem. As he did so Mel thought she heard a faint, slightly eerie murmuring . . .

Frowning, she wandered along the corridor, trying to locate its source . . . As she reached the air duct – the murmuring abruptly ceased.

'Did you hear that?'

'Er – what? No. Give me your shoe.'

Although thrown by the unusual request, she complied, tugging off her high-heeled calf-length boot. Retracing his steps to where he had noticed a fire alarm box, the Doctor smashed its glass with the boot's steel heel.

The clamour of warning bells rang, deafeningly, all over the ship!

Flipping the boot over his shoulder for Mel to catch,

the Doctor confiscated a couple of smoke masks and an axe from the array of fire-fighting equipment.

Accompanied by the raucous jangling, he dashed to the sentry. 'The lounge!' he yelled, thrusting the axe at him. 'There are passengers trapped!'

Flummoxed, the sentry hesitated.

'Quickly, man! On the double! Lives are at stake!'

The hoax succeeded and the gulled dupe ran for the lounge. Tossing Mel a smoke mask, the Doctor donned his own and nipped into the isolation room.

The room was in darkness. Groping for the light, the Doctor switched on.

An oxygen tent shrouded the bed. But unlike an orthodox, transparent oxygen tent, this consisted of opaque, plastic drapes.

With only their eyes visible above the smoke masks, the interlopers exchanged a puzzled look. Never loathe to satisfy his curiosity, the Doctor unzipped the black tent.

Light illuminated the patient.

And what a patient.

On the pillow lay a once-human face. But now it was grotesquely latticed with straggly creepers, vines, and waxy, olive leaves. Across the forehead, a stem pulsated sickeningly.

Revolted by the sight, Mel nevertheless could not resist leaning nearer – the scaly eyelids snapped open – and bony, waxy, leaf-veined hands reached for her throat!

13

Quirky Phenomena

Mel screamed and recoiled as the mutant clawed for her throat.

'No . . . No . . .' The hoarse, rasping protest came from the mutant. Toppling the oxygen tent, the verdant figure lurched from the bed.

Unmistakably human in origin, the arms and body had stems and leaves growing from their veins. But what made the aberration even more repellant was that the stems pulsated as green liquid throbbed along them.

The Doctor yanked Mel clear, placing himself between his young companion and the threat. But the mutant, staggering unsteadily, lunged not for them but for the door.

'No . . . Stop her . . .' it croaked.

Sharing Mel's horror, the Doctor was nevertheless perplexed.

'Stop Lasky . . .'

Stop Lasky? Distorted though the voice was, that name was quite audible. 'Stop Lasky –'

The door crashed wide and Lasky herself burst in followed by Doland and Bruchner.

Elbowing the Doctor and Mel aside, Bruchner grappled with the mutant while Lasky diverted to a wall cabinet. Snatching up a padded muzzle with an aerosol attached, she thrust it over the mutant's mouth.

'Get them out of here!' muttered Lasky.

Doland responded immediately, ushering the trespassers towards the door. Mel needed no second bidding but the Doctor attempted to linger.

'Out!' ordered Doland, shoving the Time Lord un-ceremoniously into the corridor.

'Stop mauling me!' The Doctor wrenched free and stripped off the smoke mask.

'I should drop the innocent party act,' advised Doland. 'Any moment now that guard you duped into believing there was a fire will be back. He's going to be even less enchanted by your antics.'

Mel removed her mask. 'Never mind the guard! That monstrosity tried to kill me!'

'Does the Commodore realise what's being isolated in there?' The Doctor emphasised the word 'isolated'.

Pausing before replying, Doland tightened the rein on his anger. 'I don't know by whose authority you ask, but if it'll put an end to your meddling, I'll explain.' He glared at Mel. 'That monstrosity, as you call her, is my lab assistant. She –'

'She!' cut in Mel.

'Ruth Baxter. We're taking her to Earth where per-haps they'll be able to reverse her condition. Our facilities on Mogar were too primitive.'

'But what happened? How did she get in that state?' Mel could not come to terms with the nightmare.

'The experimental nature of our work entails some calculated risks.'

'Calculated!' The Doctor's disgust erupted. 'You're admitting that sad travesty was a statistical probability!'

'The word should be "criminal"!' added Mel.

'Very well, I should have said unforeseen.' Doland was becoming more and more irritated with these two non-scientists who did not understand the ethics of his profession. However, he realised he had to pacify them in order to prevent them from taking further action. 'During a particularly delicate cross-fertilisation, a

79

speck of pollen penetrated a minute scratch on my assistant's thumb. She should never have left it uncovered –'

'There he is, Mister Rudge!' Preceding Rudge, the hoodwinked sentry had returned from the lounge.

Hastily, the Doctor opted for retreat.

'Halt or I'll fire!' Unholstering his phaser, the sentry took aim. There was no doubting his zeal.

The Doctor came to heel.

'Oh, Doctor, you do have the knack of landing yourself in hot water.' Shaking his head benignly, Rudge eased past the sentry.

' "Satiable curtiosity", like the Elephant's Child.'

'Never mind the *Just So* stories!' Mel knew her Rudyard Kipling from school days. 'That guard looks trigger-happy to me!'

He did.

'Simply doing his duty, Miss.' The word 'duty' tripped frequently from Rudge's tongue. 'The regulations are quite specific. Any person setting off a false alarm on an intergalactic liner is to be arrested. Forthwith.'

'There's no need to quote the book. I can explain.'

Even Mel was dumbfounded. She had every faith in the Doctor's ability to fabricate excuses, but how was he going to explain this act away? She was to be disappointed.

'Not to me.' Rudge's unctuous smile accompanied his triumph. 'To the Commodore! He is expecting you.' He gestured to the sentry. 'Take him!'

*　　*　　*

'Halt the Matrix!' The Valeyard was on his feet. 'I fail to comprehend this evidence. The Doctor is on trial for his life. Yet in his defence – a defence that is supposed to

80

prove him not guilty of the charge of meddling – he presents us with a situation in which he is deliberately flouting accepted authority.'

The elderly Guardians of the Law began to mutter sympathetic comments.

'Much of the evidence does seem to contradict your stated aim, Doctor.' The Inquisitor's contribution was put calmly, although her disapproval of the support being accorded to the prosecutor by what should have been an impartial gathering, was manifest. 'Are you claiming the Matrix is again being falsified?'

'No. And if the Valeyard would exercise the restraint that I showed during the presentation of his case against me –'

'Huh!'

'– *and* could suppress his blood lust –'

'Doctor!' The Inquisitor's patience was not limitless. 'This Court is dedicated to giving you a fair trial. Do not abuse its indulgence.'

'My apologies.'

'The Matrix, Doctor. I suggest we return to the *Hyperion III*.'

*   *   *

The *Hyperion III* was skirting the edge of a giant whirlpool, the hub of which was a Stygian blackness. Even the surrounding cosmos had undergone a slightly sinister change . . .

Seated at the console, the Commodore was contemplating the massive whirlpool through the navigational window.

'Bring us in closer,' he instructed the Deck Officer. 'Reduce the margin by a factor of point-nought-one, to point-nought-two.'

'Very narrow margin of safety, Commodore.' This

was the Doctor speaking. He had arrived with the escorting sentry.

'Not for a ship of the *Hyperion* class,' replied the Commodore.

'Still unwise,' insisted the Doctor. 'Quirky phenomena, Black Holes. They can gulp with unpredictable turbulence.'

'When I want your advice, I'll ask for it!' That was the Doctor dispensed with. He dismissed the sentry with a curt wave. 'I'll handle this. Get back on duty.'

The sentry obeyed smartly.

'What I *do* want to hear from you, Doctor, is the reason why I shouldn't toss you in the brig! Fire alarms are not playthings for irresponsible buffoons!'

While the Doctor was receiving a verbal larruping from the Commodore, Janet was experiencing panic.

The fire alarm had meant that all passengers had assembled in the lounge. This was obligatory drill. The hoax having been quickly discovered, the gathering had dispersed. But Janet had noticed a missing passenger.

'Mister Rudge,' she called as she saw Rudge in the corridor with Mel. 'Mister Rudge!'

'Steady on, Janet,' he uttered in his usual avuncular timbre.

'It's Mister Kimber, the elderly passenger in Cabin Ten. He didn't report to the fire assembly point and he's not in his cabin!'

Rudge was far from bothered. Perhaps the old boy was a bit deaf or a bit obstinate. Elderly people did not always abide by the rules.

But Janet would not be assuaged. She urged the Security Officer towards Cabin Ten.

Mel went too.

Nothing had been disturbed in the cabin.

'He hasn't touched the drink I brought him.'

Rudge shrugged. 'Well, maybe he's just wandered off. Absent-minded.'

'Without his coat?' exclaimed Janet. The jacket hung neatly in the wardrobe. 'Or his watch?'

This did strike Rudge as strange. 'When did you last see him?'

'I didn't. See him, that is. He was in the shower. I spoke to him through the door.'

Patting Janet consolingly on the shoulder, Rudge opened the bathroom divider . . .

14

The Enemy Within

The bathroom was deserted.

Apart from a residue of water in the shower and splashes on the tiles, there was no indication that Mister Kimber or his assailant had been in there.

'Where can he be? With all these killings –!'

'That'll do, Janet.' Rudge refused to tolerate histrionics. 'Pull yourself together. Going to pieces won't help. We'll search the passenger quarters before we start assuming the worst.'

With Janet in tow, he exited, brushing past Mel.

About to follow, she lingered. Something nagged. Another disappearance? The investigation needed a fresh approach. But what? She fingered the wristwatch. An inscription on its case read: *With you every second. Peter and family.* The stewardess was right. Mister Kimber wouldn't voluntarily have gone anywhere without his keepsake.

She peered into the bathroom. Initially it yielded no clue – but wait! The old man was supposed to have been taking a shower . . . yet the fluffy bath towel was folded on the shelf. Crisp and dry. Not even damp.

A positive deduction that spurred her on to examine the bathroom more keenly . . . and to discover an object not in keeping with the sterile surroundings. Attached to the air grille, caught by its stem, was a waxy, olive-green leaf.

Two waxy, olive-green arms were humping the lifeless

Kimber between the inner and outer shells of the space ship's bulkhead.

Laboured breathing accompanied the grim journey as the corpse was lugged clumsily towards a lattice-work of truss and transverse girders. Although not constructed for this purpose, the girders formed a cage.

The breathing became more stertorous and the two arms flexed and braced to tip the body into the makeshift cage . . . rolling it on top of the corpses of the electrocuted Edwardes and the guard who had found him.

Its ghoulish task completed, the creature stretched to full height. Walking upright, the biped's head was sculpted like a closed ivory brown bud. It had sunken cheeks that projected forward an o-shaped, rubbery mouth. Curling, transparent sepals shielded ear-slits. Neither eyebrows nor lashes framed the lidless, staring eyes in the grotesque, noseless face. Noseless because, like plants, it breathed through its waxy leaves.

As it advanced, shuffling, it gazed approvingly at the makeshift cage, then patted its green arms with congratulatory fervour . . . The only sound was the rustling of the leaves that grew all over its body and from the arms and legs.

This was a Vervoid.

One of the creatures that had been able to emerge from the giant shucks after the impact of high intensity light.

Approvingly, it crushed the three humans together as though making room for more, before shufflling away again along the narrow duct leading from the bulkhead and the cage . . .

'A grim picture, Doctor.'

An apt comment from the Commodore who had just been given a description of the mutant in the isolation room.

'I've no reason to lie, Commodore.'

'And I'm not questioning your honesty. Simply your methods. However, I'm left with little alternative but to begin to co-operate.'

'Begin? I take it you mean, begin *overtly* to co-operate.'

'This could be the shortest alliance on record! You'd do well to remember I'm in command here!'

'Commodore, you've been using me. I would never have been allowed to run free if you hadn't condoned it!'

The Commodore's eyes twinkled as he met the Doctor's gaze. 'Fair comment. So shall we dispense with the fencing?'

'Agreed.' But the Doctor wasn't finished. 'Frankly, I think you should report the death of the investigator Hallet to the authorities on Earth and insist on being given details of his mission.' The Time Lord knew if they could discover what Hallet was meant to be investigating on the ship, they would have a lead to the murderer . . . and to any other mystery aboard.

'You underestimate me to that extent, do you?'

'Sorry. They refused?'

'Top secret. By the time they've gone through channels, we'll probaby have docked!'

'That can't happen!' Instinct told the Doctor that whatever evil existed must be confined to the *Hyperion III*.

'No-one will be allowed to disembark. The murderer won't escape.'

'The murderer . . . yes . . .' Abruptly he turned to leave. Second thoughts. 'You'll tell me as soon as you get a reply, Commodore?'

'Certainly, Doctor. I'll match you for candour. . . .'

The ambiguity of the reply did not miss the Doctor as

he departed.

Robbed even of his pomposity, Rudge's ambience would have suited Uriah Heep rather than that of a superior officer as he came into the lounge.

'Did you find Mister Kimber?' Janet kept her voice low. Atza and Ortezo, although some distance away, were seated at a table.

'Not a sign. You?'

She shook her head.

'I'll have to report we've lost another passenger. That'll improve the Commodore's temper, I'll guarantee!' he said and made for the exit.

Atza rose from his recliner. 'Mister Rudge!'

'Later.' Rudge did not pause.

'Come here!' This was not a request from Atza: it was an order! Made in such a peremptory fashion that the Security Officer should have objected.

He did not.

Instead, he hesitated, then diverted to where the two Mogarians waited.

'We want to know what is happening,' Atza said.

'Yes. Where was the fire?' Ortezo joined in.

'It was a false alarm. Nothing to worry about. You'll have to excuse me. I've urgent things to do.'

'Sit down, Rudge! There is only one thing you have got to do!'

'That is to tell us exactly what is going on!' Ortezo commanded.

Before sitting, Rudge self-consciously checked to see if Janet had overheard the telling exchange.

Ignoring this, Atza delivered the final mandate. 'And I suggest you begin telling us right now!'

Fear is a contagion; an emotional virus. Imperceptibly, with enervating stealth, it spreads, eroding the fortitude of even the most stalwart.

Infected by the insidious malaise, the sentry outside the isolation room shifted uneasily. An irresistible combination of sounds was undermining his resolve. In sequence they were a metallic clinking, a vague shuffling, and a door hinge creaking.

He had to know the cause. Therefore, risking reprimand, the sentry abandoned his post and sauntered to the corner.

No one was in the corridor . . . But an air duct grille was unlatched . . . and swinging gently on the recycled currents of air. Little did he know it was the duct from which Mel had heard eerie murmurs while the Doctor was concocting his deceptive fire alarm caper.

Intrigued, the sentry took the fateful steps to inspect the grille . . . But before he could peer in – a Vervoid shuffled from the adjacent cabin . . .

Awestricken by this grotesque apparition, the man's training took over. Frantically tapping in a code, he raised the communicator to his lips to summon help – a waxy, olive, leaf-veined hand darted from the air duct and shot a stinging thorn into his cheek.

'*Yes?*' The Commodore's voice echoed through the communicator.

No reply to the question was received on the bridge. Only the wheezing gasps of choking came back . . .

'*What is it?*' Perplexed, the Commander leant closer – to the intercom.

'*State your position!*' The disembodied instruction filtering from the communicator fell on dead ears. Poisoned by the lethal thorn, the sentry had collapsed to the floor.

'Quickly,' the attacking Vervoid called to its cohort. 'Help me with this.' The voice, in a minor key, was dominated by a hissing since consonants took preference over vowels.

Between them, the Vervoids gathered up the dead sentry and bundled him into the duct, treading on the communicator in the process.

Static crackled discordantly on the bridge as the communicator broke.

'What the blazes was that?' The Commodore flicked off the intercom. 'Trace that call!' he instructed the Duty Officer.

Swivelling the command chair, the Commodore rose and went to the concave navigational window. Leaning forward, knuckles resting on the sill, he gazed out at the unfriendly vacuum of space. Most of his adult life had been spent traversing this celestial ocean with its impersonal hostility, and, from the beginning, he had never managed to shake off the feeling of vulnerability. Not that he would admit it. The garbled voice on the intercom brought home the new dimension to his vulnerability: the enemy was within.

Broadly, he had two options. To mount an assault; pull every available man from his post and organise a detailed search. There was an almost overwhelming attraction to pursue this positive path, yet he knew that with all the ship's personnel, a search of the huge intricate ship could not be completed before they docked.

The other option would be to keep the crew on red alert, which had the crucial benefit of providing the passengers with a greater degree of protection.

However, events were about to make the Solomon-like ponderings racking the Commodore superfluous – catastrophically so . . .

15

Deadly Disposal

Defence may have been the Commodore's choice but not Bruchner's. The scientist had taken a violent initiative. One that aroused fierce indignation in Doland. What he saw in the hydroponic work hut was tantamount to treason. Bruchner was destroying the notes and papers of their experiments.

'Have you gone out of your mind, Bruchner?' Doland was aghast as he viewed the devastation.

'I have been. But not any more. I've regained my sanity.' In contrast to the havoc he had wrought, Bruchner was calm; unnaturally so.

Doland wanted to wrench the precious notebooks away. They represented years of research. However, he was wise enough to realise any arbitrary move on his part would just inflame the situation.

He tried reasoning. 'It's not only your own work you're destroying. Other people have contributed. You have no right to do this.'

'You long ago lost sight of the difference between right and wrong,' retorted Bruchner as he ripped more pages into shreds.

'Why? Because of some unexplained incidents?'

'On my way down here, I heard of another "unexplained incident". From the stewardess. That harmless old man is missing . . . How many more, Doland, before you and Lasky accept responsibility?'

Stepping out of the hut, Doland turned the key,

locking Bruchner inside, then hurried off to find Lasky: she could deal with her recalcitrant assistant!

'I'm far too busy for a horticultural dissertation, young woman,' Lasky barked at Mel. As was her practice, the large-boned but trim-figured professor was taking her ritual exercise in the gym. 'The activities of you and your erratic friend have already disrupted my routine.' She pedalled furiously, notching up mileage on the tachometer.

Not put off, Mel held out the leaf she found stuck in the bathroom grille. 'I only asked if you'd tell me what this leaf is.'

'After my work-out. And that's final!'

Obduracy was hardly a characteristic Mel could reasonably object to, being amply endowed with the same quality herself. She withdrew temporarily to the vionesium sunbed to await the granting of an audience with the autocratic academic.

Doland burst in.

Glancing at Mel, his tone was hushed as he appealed to Lasky. 'Can I speak to you privately?'

'Really! But now, Doland!' He got short shrift too!

Normally he would have deferred to her wishes. However the urgency of the matter emboldened him. 'I know you object to your schedule being interrupted, but this is extremey vital.'

'Well?' She did not stop pedalling.

'It's important you –' he was very aware of Mel's presence in the vicinity – 'speak to Bruchner. Er – calm him down.'

'Can't you?'

'He won't listen to me.'

'Where is he?' Lasky dismounted from the exercise bike.

'Locked in the work hut.'

'Then leave him there to cool off. I'll talk to him later.' Sighing with exasperation, she petulantly snatched a length of paper towelling from a dispenser. 'Perhaps I can get some peace in my cabin!'

Swabbing her face, she flung the screwed-up towelling into a large disposal bin on wheels and stomped from the gym.

'Er – Mister Doland' – this was Mel – 'Let's pick up where we broke off, shall we?' She was thinking of the discussion they had had after the discovery of the mutant, Ruth Baxter, in the isolation room. 'While you're in the mood for explanations.'

'Did I give you that impression?' came the non-committal reply.

'What are those pods in the hydroponic centre?' Typical Mel. Straight to the point. No dancing about.

'The result of another experiment.' An oblique answer.

'I could've made an educated guess at that! What was in them?'

'Giant fruit. And, anticipating your next question, we left them on Mogar.' He began to move off. 'We're merely taking the shucks as an example for fellow agronomists in Earth-bound laboratories.'

Mel glared after his departing figure. 'I hope he's a better scientist than he is a liar.' she muttered to herself.

About to quit the gym, she halted.

An eerie, murmuring was filtering in . . . and it seemed to be coming from the air duct high above the parallel wallbars . . .

Nimbly, she scaled the wallbars, then strained against the grille, trying to hear more clearly.

But the murmurings remained indistinct.

Hanging on, arm crooked through the top bar, she looked around in frustration. If only she could amplify the murmurings – inspiration!

In a flurry of explosive agility, she descended the bars, snatched a portable two-way headset with a throat mike from the shelf, and reascended the rungs.

Feverishly, she hooked the headset to the grille, poking the mike through the slats. Then, leaping to the ground, she hared into the observation cubicle.

Fingers twitching, she contemplated the audio apparatus. 'Think! Think!' Anxiety was inhibiting her from sorting out the correct procedure.

She jabbed several buttons. Tiny lights flashed but no sound emerged. 'Less haste . . . amplifier . . . amplifier . . .' That's what she was seeking. If she could amplify the murmurings, she would be able to hear what was being said.

She tried another control. Voices. Too faint. She increased the volume –

' – *reckless actions! We must not make animalkind aware of our existence. Not yet. They still outnumber us. If we are to kill them all – and we shall – we must hunt them down secretly . . .*'

Mel's mouth gaped with horror as she listened to the sibilant whisperings. This reflex was an unexpected bonus for someone . . .

Someone who had stolen into the observation room . . . Whose gloved hands thrust a muzzle with an aerosol attached over Mel's parted lips . . .

She managed only a suppressed scream before succumbing to the anaesthetizing gas. . . .

' "*Is there anybody there?* said the traveller",' the Doctor quoted from Walter de la Mare. His delivery was perfect. A pity there was no-one to appreciate it in the deserted lounge.

'Perhaps she's in the gym.'

She was.

But not performing aerobics . . . or skipping . . . or pedalling on the exercise bike. Comatose, Mel had been buried beneath layers of crumpled paper towelling in the wheeled wastebin. The question the Doctor had posed was less than apposite: Mel's destiny rather than her whereabouts was more relevant.

Humming tunelessly, shoving a train of wastebins, a rubbish collector clattered into the gym. He swapped 126, the bin containing Mel, with a pristine replacement.

'Allow me.' With a friendly grin, the Doctor, entering, held the door ajar for the rubbish collector and his wagon-train to exit.

A courteous gesture that sped Mel on her way to a grisly disposal.

16

A Heinous Crime

In his quest for Mel, the Doctor poked his head into the observation cubicle . . . and noticed the audio deck tape spinning on record.

Curiosity to the fore, he rewound the tape and activated the reply: '– *reckless actions. We must not make animalkind aware of our existence . . .*'

The sibilant message of hate that had confounded Mel was repeated for the Doctor.

Gloom had settled upon the rubbish collector as he plodded into an elevator and descended to a lower deck. He no longer hummed his tuneless song. The good-natured repartee that invariably sparked between himself and passing crew members was absent: the red alert was curbing the usual bonhomie.

Coupling fresh bins to his train, he trudged on, oblivious to the fact that in bin 126 lay the anaesthetized Mel. Her erstwhile assailant had cast the innocent collector in the role of an accomplice to murder. . . .

'. . . *to kill them all – and we shall – we must hunt them down secretly.*'

If these sentiments disturbed the Doctor, the next sound from the tape appalled him.

It was Mel's stifled scream.

He also recognised and understood the import of the sequence that followed, which culminated in his own 'Allow me' to the exiting rubbish collector!

On wings of desperation, he gave chase.

'The wastebins! Where do they go?'

Janet blinked at the distraught Doctor in apparent bewilderment as he burst into the lounge.

'Wastebins?'

'Quickly, woman! Where are they taken?'

'The pulveriser. Why do you want –'

She was alone again!

A line of wastebins, including 126, abutted the pulveriser. In fairly rapid succession, the bins were upended and rammed against the iris-shaped shutter.

The rapacious jaws opened and the bins' contents were sucked into the mincing blades to be fragmented and spewed into space. Under the expert manipulation of the operator, each bin was evacuated in mere seconds.

Inexorably Mel's bin trundled closer . . . closer . . . then the wait was over . . . 126 rolled into position . . . With practised economy, the operator tipped the lid and grasped its sides –

'*Stop!*'

Pell-mell, the Doctor dashed into the disposal unit and flung himself upon bin 126!

Yanking it from the operator's grasp, he burrowed beneath the tangle of paper towelling.

There lay Mel in blissful repose . . .

Her dark-fringed eyelashes fluttered and she smiled drowsily at her rescuer.

Relief brought an groan-worthy pun from the Time Lord. 'Don't throw in the towel, Mel!'

In contrast with Mel's tranquilised mood, turbulence dominated the navigational window on the bridge. The spiralling tentacles of the Black Hole of Tartarus curled ominously as the *Hyperion III* got closer.

However, the Commodore glowered not at the Black Hole but at the contrite Rudge who had just brought news of Mister Kimber's disappearance.

'Why in Hades haven't you reported before now? As a Security Officer you're an unmitigated disaster!'

'That's hardly fair –'

'Silence!' The Commodore bridled. 'We've had a passenger murdered. According to you, another's disappeared. Three members of the crew are missing, unaccounted for. And you haven't a clue as to why they've gone or where they are!'

To be just to Rudge, he could not know.

Nor could anyone else.

Not unless they made a habit of crawling through the air vents to the bulkhead where Vervoids were milling about.

The corpse of the sentry from outside the isolation cabin was being added to that of Mister Kimber and the earlier victims in the improvised cage.

'We are doing splendidly,' hissed the First Vervoid, surveying the pathetic pile of bodies.

'Congratulations must be delayed until that is full,' cautioned the Second Vervoid.

The First Vervoid nodded approvingly. 'We shall not have long to wait . . .'

'It's gone!'

'What has?'

'The tape.' The Doctor was scrabbling among the tape stacks in the observation cubicle. 'The proof we need to force Lasky's hand.'

'The killer's obviously removed it.'

'Just as he tried to remove you.' Mentally the Doctor had a vision of the chomping pulveriser and the end his

97

companion so nearly suffered.

'He?' picked up Mel. 'Why not she?'

This thought had not struck the Doctor. 'Lasky?'

'Or the stewardess, Janet.'

'Janet?' Incredulity tinged the reply.

'Wouldn't've taken a man's strength to lift my weight. A woman could've dumped me in the waste-bin.' Perfectly true. Petite and slender, Mel would have been no weight to lift.

Considering this fact, the Doctor entered the gym and, puffing, clambered up the wallbars. Mel, more sprightly, climbed up beside him.

He peered into the duct. 'What are they? And how do they link with these murders?'

'Whatever they are, they're not human! We're all to be destroyed, remember?'

'Still got that piece of leaf?' he asked as they descended.

Mel produced the leaf she had found in Mister Kimber's bathroom. The Doctor compared it with the leaf he had taken from Hallet's pocket: the one Hallet had discovered in the hydroponic centre when he was masquerading as a Mogarian.

Abruptly, the Time Lord turned to leave.

'Where're you off to?'

'Hydroponic centre. There has to be a connection.'

'What about me?'

'Follow your own theory. See if Janet's got the tape.' He paused. 'But, Mel, be careful . . .' His concern for the spirited diminutive redhead was genuine.

'You too, Doctor.' She was equally concerned.

They parted to go their separate ways.

* * *

However, on the Matrix screen the Doctor's colourful

98

figure could next be seen not in the hydroponic centre, but in the communications room where, unbelievably, he had launched into a ruthless and systematic demolition of the equipment! Transmitters and receivers were reduced to scrap as the Doctor, in the style of a rampant Dervish, chopped at them with an axe!

'I didn't do that!' The Doctor clenched the rail of the prisoner's dock.

'Stop the Matrix,' the Inquisitor commanded.

Exaggeratedly world-weary, the Valeyard took up the cudgel. 'Are we to be subjected to more chicanery, Sagacity?'

'It wasn't me in there!' protested the Doctor.

'Ridiculous! We all saw you. You're scarcely mistakable in that outfit.'

'I didn't smash the equipment.'

The Inquisitor intervened. 'Are you saying, Doctor, the communications equipment was not sabotaged?'

'No. It had to be to prevent the Commodore getting information from Earth. But I didn't do it.'

'Then who did?' she asked.

'The murderer.'

'The murderer?' the Valeyard repeated. 'I think, Inquisitor, the Doctor is telling us more than he realises . . .'

'The prosecutor delights in scoring cheap victories, my Lady,' responded the Doctor scornfully. 'But I swear to you when I reviewed this section earlier in preparing my defence, I was nowhere near that communications room.'

'So once again the defendant is accusing the Matrix of being wrong,' came the Valeyard's sarcastic dismissal.

'Are you, Doctor?' queried the Inquisitor.

'Yes. Yes, I am.'

'If you're questioning its veracity, is there any value in continuing with the Matrix?' she persisted.

'What else have I got? Without evidence to prove my innocence, I'm condemned.'

This was too good an opportunity for Valeyard to miss. 'And *with* it you are condemned it seems, Doctor . . . Shall we continue?'

The Doctor looked contemplatively at the Valeyard. Disputed though the claim may be, he knew the sacred Matrix had been violated. By whom or for what purpose, he failed to comprehend. Surely the execution of a Time Lord, serious as that would be, hardly warranted such a heinous crime.

17

The Black Hole of Tartarus

'Let's hope we don't need to call for outside help!' The Commodore surveyed the shambles in the communications room.

The Doctor may have maintained to the Time Lords that he did not wreak the havoc, but someone had done a thorough job. The Commodore toed a shattered magnetron. 'There's no way we can repair that!' he said to the Duty Officer accompanying him. 'We're completely isolated!' He kicked the ruined component into the centre of the ravaged circuitry, and stormed off.

'Sheer vandalism. And utterly useless!' Lasky had eventually gone to the work hut to deal with her incarcerated assistant.

A pyre of disintegrating grey ash was all that remained of the years of experimentation which had gone into the creation of the Vervoids.

Burning the notes had acted as a catharsis for Bruchner. 'Is that how you see it, Professor?'

'How else?'

'Because I've put an end to this obscene experiment? Someone had to.'

'I should imagine when man first discovered fire, there were those who were equally dismayed and wanted it suppressed. If they'd prevailed, the human race would still be cowering in caves.'

(These irate polemics had a pertinent eavesdropper . . . From the interior of an air vent in the cargo hold, the First Vervoid strained to hear . . .)

'To use your own phrase, Professor, that is entirely academic now.'

Distressed as she was, Lasky could appreciate the heartfelt passion that possessed the tormented conscience of her colleague. 'Bruchner, if you were rational, you'd realise how pointless this is. We can't unlearn knowledge.'

The statement seemed to penetrate Bruchner's cocoon of certitude. He frowned.

Hopeful that she was getting through, Lasky continued. 'You're not illiterate. How often has a great advance produced this reaction? Think of Galileo.' She was referring to the Italian genius born in the Earth year 1546 who was imprisoned in a futile attempt to suppress his scientific discoveries.

'Galileo? Is that it? You see the name Lasky inscribed in the history books?'

'Nonsense!' Lasky was in danger of losing her composure. 'This has been a team effort.'

'With you as leader.'

The taunt puzzled her.

'Well, you've fulfilled that role to the last. You've led me to see the fault in my strategy.' His hand was closing about a spar of wood from a dismantled shelf. 'You. Me. Doland. Even the creatures we've spawned. The sole representatives of this great advance.'

(At the grille, the Vervoid turned its face into a noseless profile, pressing its flapped ear against the mesh . . .)

'And we're all encapsulated in this ship . . . In this ship!' Giving Lasky no chance to deflect the blow, Bruchner clouted her with the spar – then ran from the hut, an objective clearly in mind. But to achieve it would require more than a wooden spar. He needed a phaser . . . and he knew where to get one . . .

The replacement sentry outside the isolation room crumpled to the ground. Politely, he had moved aside to allow Bruchner access to the unfortunate Ruth Baxter. The attack, when it came, had been completely unexpected.

Equipped with the sentry's phaser, Bruchner continued along the corridor . . . and into danger – a Vervoid arm lunged from the air duct!

In reflex, Bruchner slammed shut the open grille severing the brittle arm.

The danger was not over.

Propelled by its sharp, thorn-like talons, the severed waxy, olive-green limb began scrabbling towards him.

He fled. Any misgivings about his drastic plan were expunged by the gruesome mutation.

'I don't care what you heard on some mythical tape!'

Lasky, propped against the work bench, was allowing the Doctor to examine her bruised forehead. She wanted only to talk of Bruchner's attack, but the Doctor, who had come to the hydroponic centre to question her about the missing tape and the mysterious voices on it, persisted.

'You're letting arrogance blinker you, Professor. Maybe it's not your intention, but you're running the risk of joining an extensive role of dishonour. Misguided scientists who've claimed the pursuit of truth as an excuse for immoral experiments.'

'There's no time to debate ethics!' retorted Lasky, scrambling to her feet. 'I made that mistake with Bruchner! I tell you the man's demented. He's out to destroy this ship. And everyone on it!'

The stolen phaser was levelled at the two officers on the bridge. 'Get out of here!' Bruchner commanded.

Instinctively the Commodore reached for the

emergency tab – an intense beam blasted from the phaser searing the Commodore's wrist, disabling him.

'Move! Now! Or I'll kill you both!' That Bruchner was capable of executing this uncompromising threat was crystal clear. Non-compliance would have been tantamount to committing suicide. Grudgingly the Commodore and Duty Officer retreated to the lobby.

On their departure, Bruchner energized a locking device, causing two heavy panels to slide together forming an impregnable barrier that sealed off the control section from the rest of the ship.

In the lobby, beyond the barrier, the Duty Officer's immediate concern was his superior's injury.

'Leave that till later. Get the laser lance up here!'

The officer hesitated.

'*Now!*' barked the Commodore. 'And bring stun guns with you!'

At the double, his subordinate left, passing Lasky and the Doctor who were entering the small ante-chamber.

'Bruchner?' she asked, indicating the sealed panels and the inflamed wound.

'Yes. Why? What's his motive?' rasped the Commodore.

'I rather think his intention is the vital question,' the Doctor corrected.

'All right. What's his –' Pain creased the handsome face. 'Just tell me, Doctor!'

'He's determined to destroy this ship.'

'And the rest of us with it,' added Lasky.

'Does the lunatic know anything about flying a space craft?' Another grimace of pain accompanied the Commodore's words.

'Bruchner's been trained as an astronaut,' informed Lasky. 'One of the team had to be. Obligatory requirement.'

'Very thorough.' The bitter sarcasm had a finality that did not bode well.

'Can the power to the bridge be cut off?' Straw-clutching was a trait of the Doctor's.

'Not a hope. It's designed to be hi-jack proof. From the outside!'

Suddenly, an almost imperceptible tremor shuddered through the lobby.

Bruchner's training had, indeed, been thorough. At the command console on the bridge, he adeptly fed in course changes, igniting the directional boosters. On the navigational window, the image of the Black Hole of Tartarus began to shift from its offset position . . . until the co-ordinate grid had the rapacious whirlpool fixed plumb centre.

Another minor adjustment, and the intergalactic liner's prow was locked into the epicentre of the beckoning Black Hole . . .

Already the cosmos's most sinister gravitational forces were sucking the craft into ever increasing speed. Thrust against the lobby wall, Lasky fought for balance. 'What's happening?'

'Isn't that obvious? We're running into turbulence!' Because of his injury, the Commodore was having even greater difficulty in maintaining his balance.

'I'd say rather more than turbulence,' stated the Doctor, solicitously steadying the Commodore.

'Don't talk in riddles, man!' Typically, Lasky gave the Doctor's ambiguity short shrift.

The Doctor hesitated, reluctant to forecast imminent death for all aboard. 'Your colleague is aiming the *Hyperion III* straight into the eye of the Black Hole of Tartarus!'

18

A Deadly Intruder

Where was Mel during the build-up of this potential calamity?

When the Doctor set off from the gym, Mel had headed unerringly for Janet's cabin in the crew's quarters to seek the missing audio tape.

Avoiding detection, she approached a door marked *STEWARDESS*, and knocked. Getting no reply, she thought her luck was in. She could not have been more wrong. Terrifyingly so.

Nipping inside, she paused, looking about to take stock.

'Can I tempt you to a coffee?' Janet asked Atza, proffering a tray.

'No, thank you.' Atza's translator blinked.

'How about you, sir?'

Ortezo, waving an expansive negative, knocked the tray, splattering the stewardess's skirt with coffee. Her flicker of annoyance was quickly superseded by a professional politeness at the Mogarian's gesture of apology. 'Not to worry. It's easily changed,' she said, inspecting the brown stains on her white and pink uniform.

Mel, too, was inspecting a white and pink uniform. Freshly laundered, it hung in Janet's wardrobe.

As she dipped into the pockets for the incriminating audio tape, there was a click . . . the door handle began slowly to revolve . . .

In disarray, Mel sought shelter in the bathroom. Closing the divider, she scrambled into the shower and pulled the curtain to, imagining she was hiding from Janet.

But the hand twisting the door knob was not Janet's. It was green, with thorns for fingernails . . .

Framed on the threshold, the prowling Vervoid seethed with anger. The creature had been certain the cabin housed a human. In frustration, it dragged the mattress from the bed. When this yielded no victim, clothes were brutally torn from their wardrobe hangers in a homicidal hunt.

The adjacent rampage disabused Mel of the belief that Janet had returned to her cabin. Cringing behind the shower curtain, she wondered how long it would be before the savage intruder located her. Once it had, she harboured no illusions of what her fate would be. She had heard the Vervoid's avowed intent to eliminate animalkind.

That same voice Mel had heard was still issuing death sentences. 'Bruchner must be stopped!'

The single lamp in the bulkhead threw shadows over the pathetic heap of human corpses: shadows which grew and shrunk as the Vervoids gathered in their lair to hear the pronouncement of their leader.

'We are unique. The only members of the Vervoid species. If Bruchner succeeds in eradicating us, Vervoids will cease to exist.' It flexed its glistening verdant torso as it scanned the assembled throng through lidless eyes. 'Forget your previous orders. Bruchner's death is now our priority. He cannot be permitted to prevent us from reaching the planet Earth.'

Grotesque, noseless heads nodded, as rubbery lips hissed in agreement.

The lone foraging Vervoid had exhausted his plundering of Janet's cabin and was now in the bathroom.

A violent judder sent it reeling against the wash-basin.

Bottles crashed from the shelf, splintering into shards of glass.

Riven by fear, the Vervoid began to snort wispy fumes of gas from its distorted mouth.

'All Vervoids to the bridge area!' The sibilant instruction echoed from the air duct. 'All Vervoids to the bridge area!'

Huffing with fear, trailing fumes in its wake, the Vervoid obeyed the summons and quit the stewardess's quarters.

Relief flooded over Mel and she stumbled from the bathroom, coughing and gasping from the effects of the suffocating gas.

But respite was to be short-lived. The *Hyperion III* bucked, sending her sprawling.

Books slithered from the tables. Beakers jingled and danced along the counter.

Janet, Rudge, Doland and the two Mogarians clutched at pillars for support as chairs skittered across the lounge.

Unlike the blenched faces of everyone else on the ship, Bruchner's was aglow with messianic elation. Dominating the navigational window, the blood-red inwardly spiralling tentacles of the Black Hole progressed through deepening purple to a sulphurous ebony . . .

19

A Whiff of Death

Fluctuating turbulence, rippling the outer shallows of the Black Hole, pounded the intergalactic liner with escalating ferocity.

Chaos dominated the lounge. Atza and Ortezo were buffeted by dislodged chairs as they clung to the reception desk. In mutual fright, Janet and Doland hung on to each other and to a pillar.

Affecting an indomitable stoicism, Rudge, staggering drunkenly, made his way to the exit. He had to get to the bridge.

The blistering ray from the laser lance was only held steady by the combined efforts of the Doctor and the Duty Officer. Progress was pitfully slow. The safety barrier to the bridge was not meant to be breached with ease.

'How long before the ship arrives at the point of no return, Commodore?' Lasky, wedged in a corner, wanted the truth, however unpalatable.

His brooding eyes shaded by drawn brows, the Commodore paused before replying. 'That's a question no-one's survived to answer!'

Nor did Bruchner intend they should create a precedent. He regretted this, for he had no wish to harm the crew, the passengers, or those with whom he had worked for years. But he knew, with every vestige of his considerable intelligence, that if the Vervoids were allowed to reach Earth, then that would be the end of humankind.

They would proliferate wherever there was fertile soil available to nourish them. Man could make a strategic withdrawal to the deserts . . . yet Bruchner realised the Vervoids were not beyond devising a means of propagating themselves even in the barren wastes.

Transfixed, clutching the console for support, the scientist was mesmerised by the spectacle of the voracious vortex. This rent in the fabric of the Universe would ingest into bone-crushing oblivion the abominations that had been so irresponsibly hatched.

Balefully, these 'abominations' glared at their adversary from every airduct ventilating the bridge. His fixation with Tartarus had kept Bruchner's attention glued to the navigational window. Had he been aware of the proximity of the Vervoids, he would not have worried: the grilles were welded fast; safety experts had seen to that.

But the frustrated creatures were not finished. The genetic engineering so assiduously manipulated by their originators had endowed them with the ability to improvise. Rubbery lips pressed against the meshed grilles and vermilion cheeks ballooned as wispy fumes of gas streamed into the bridge. Almost languidly, the gas shrouded the scientist.

The result was inevitable. Bruchner's death wish was about to be fulfilled . . .

Negotiating swaying corridors, Rudge attained the antechamber just as the laser lance completed a circular incision in the barrier.

At a nod from the Commodore, the lock was punched out. Immediately, fetid fumes spewed through. With commendable presence of mind, the Duty Officer stuffed his jacket into the hole, blocking off the rancid gas.

The minuscule quantity of fumes had reduced all in the antechamber to incoherent spluttering and choking.

Bruchner, however, was beyond that.

Lungs corrupted by the vapour, he lay lifelessly across the control console. The Vervoids had succeeded in killing him, but they had failed to abort his objective: the pilotless *Hyperion III* was unwaveringly plunging to destruction.

'Marsh gas?' gasped the Doctor, the first to recover breath.

'A methane derivative.' Coughing or not, Lasky was going to be precise.

'Marsh gas!' exploded the Commodore. 'Where the devil's that come from? What is it you two know that I don't?'

A din of groaning metal punctuated his demand as the ship's superstructure was taxed by stress.

'Explanations later.' For the Doctor to eschew debate was a measure of their peril. 'Would smoke masks protect?' he asked Lasky.

'No, they'd be completely inadequate.'

'Are you saying none of us can go in there?'

'It'd be suicidal.'

Obdurately, the Commodore, nursing his injured arm, lurched towards the barrier.

'No. Let me, Commodore.' Quixotic gestures were the Doctor's prerogative.

'It's my ship. If there's a risk to be taken, I'll take it!'

Coolly, Rudge resolved the argument. 'There's no need for heroics from either of you.'

His blandness puzzled them. So did his next action. He switched on his communicator and contacted the lounge.

111

20

Hijack

A cacophony of protesting metal heralded the bucking tremor that toppled Bruchner from the console.

Through the dense pall of Vervoid gas enveloping the bridge, two figures began to take shape. They wore protective silver suits topped by begoggled helmets. Astutely, Rudge had sent for the only individuals aboard equipped to deal with the crisis. The Mogarians.

Grasping the command chairs for support, Atza and Ortezo began trying feverishly to override the instructions Bruchner had fed into the guidance system.

'If they make a hash of it in there, we're finished!' Stating the obvious was a measure of the Commodore's sense of impotence.

'Oh, I doubt that will happen, sir,' replied Rudge in the bland tone he had adopted since his arrival in the antechamber. He smiled confidently at Lasky.

The Security Officer's self-assurance perplexed the Doctor. That Rudge was a weak person, he had no doubt, yet, with catastrophe a hair's breadth away, the man was relaxed and lacking in fear.

Helmets uplifted, the Mogarians watched the malignant whirlpool filling the window to space. They had done everything possible. All they could do now was wait and hope that it was not too late.

The unabating racket assumed a deafening volume as the great ship's fabric bore the brunt of the stresses imposed by the change of course. Gradually, agonisingly so, the prow of the *Hyperion III* angled away from Tartarus and the plunge into the swirling void was reversed.

Gloating equanimity oozed from Rudge. His optimism regarding the skill of the Mogarians had been confirmed.

While sharing the general relief, the Doctor was nevertheless still troubled by the attitude of the Security Officer. Was there more to the overweening smugness? How did he know so much about the two aliens?

The answers would come when the barriers to the bridge were unsealed. This already eventful voyage was far from calm waters . . .

*　　*　　*

The Valeyard, too, was ruffling troubled waters. 'The mortality rate that attends your meddling, Doctor, is appalling.'

'You hold me responsible for Bruchner's death?'

'Can you nominate a single incident where your presence has stemmed the tide of disaster?'

The Inquisitor interrupted. 'Are you arguing that the submission for the defence should be curtailed?'

'A sentence of guilty can be the only conclusion.'

'Sit down, Valeyard! In my Court, *I* decide the verdict!'

Contritely, the prosecutor obeyed. Antagonising the Inquisitor would have been maladroit. She must get the impression it was the Doctor who was abusing her indulgence. Undermining the defence must be the game plan.

'The quick thinking of the man Rudge seemed to disturb you, Doctor.'

The Doctor nodded as he reviewed, in his mind, the events that were to come. 'Yes, my Lady. Unfortunately my misgivings were justified . . .'

Fussing unnecessarily, she adjusted her crimson sash: a habit that indicated a lapse into introspection. She pondered the Doctor's assertion. Did that mean Rudge was the murderer? He was on her list of suspects. But then, so, also, was Lasky. Despite her solemn responsibility to the case before her, the Inquisitor had become intrigued with the whodunnit aspect of the Doctor's story.

*　　*　　*

Having steered the *Hyperion* back on course and cleared the bridge of the lethal fumes, Atza and Ortezo disengaged the sealed panels.

'I'm grateful to you both,' said the Commodore coming forward to greet them. 'Now, if the air is breathable, I'll resume command.'

'I'm afraid that isn't going to be possible, Commodore.' Rudge underlined his announcement by levelling his phaser.

'What Rudge is stating, in the usual devious manner of humans, is that we are taking over the ship,' informed Atza.

'A hijack?' Rudge's *volte-face* came as less of a surprise to the Doctor than did the participation of the Mogarians. 'You Mogarians are a peace-loving race. Violence is repugnant to you.'

'No-one will be harmed if they obey orders.' Atza's pledge was genuine.

So was the Commodore's: 'Rudge, I'll personally see to it that you rot in jail!'

Civility vanished: the frustration that had been festering in Rudge erupted. 'I should restrain that tongue of yours, Commodore,' he sneered. 'The Mogarians may shun violence, but I don't share their qualms. All my life there's been someone like you patronizing me. Treating me with contempt. I'd welcome the opportunity of settling the score!'

Before the Commodore could accept the challenge, Atza intervened. 'Mister Rudge, take the hostages to the passenger lounge!'

Unaware that her domain was about to become a prison, Janet busied herself salvaging the beakers and plates littering the floor of the lounge.

His usual imperturbability absent, Doland fretted impatiently. 'Surely you can contact the bridge now!'

'They're not responding, Mister Doland. I've just tried.'

Now the maelstrom had abated, Mel, less supine than the stewardess, was seeking the Doctor. She may not have recovered the audio tape but she had quite a tale to tell.

Trotting along a corridor, she breezed round a corner and spotted the captive party at the other end.

Reacting with commendable nimbleness, the Doctor, in the van of the group, spun about and flung his arms wide. 'Hold on, Rudge!' His remonstration was needlessly loud. 'If we're being hijacked, we deserve an explanation.'

'Any more unexpected moves and it won't be an explanation you'll get!' Rudge, in the rear, phaser at the ready, had not seen Mel.

'I wouldn't've thought I was being unreasonable.' The Doctor's 'protest' achieved the desired result: undetected, Mel beat a mercurial retreat.

'We're being hijacked!' Mel's dramatic arrival in the lounge momentarily disorientated Janet and Doland. 'If you don't want to be caught, come on!' All said without

115

pause as she hared through the far exit.

The appeal to self-preservation prevailed: Janet and Doland thrust aside their confused doubts and followed.

As one door shut, another opened.

The Doctor, leading the hostages into the lounge, attempted to take up a position near the far exit.

'No, Doctor. That end.' Patronisingly Rudge indicated mid-room, away from the door. 'Then you won't be tempted to try anything stupid.' He held out his hand to the Commodore. 'I'll have the keys to the vault.'

'The blazes you will –'

With an alacrity that suggested this was what he had been longing to do, Rudge clubbed the injured Commodore and knocked him to the ground. 'Stay back!' He flourished the phaser at the Doctor and the Duty Officer, then spoke to Lasky. 'Reach into the Commodore's pocket and take the keys out . . . carefully . . .'

'What is it you want from the vault?' The Doctor had been studying Rudge keenly.

'Me? Not a thing.' Magnanimously, the Security Officer was prepared to humour his captives. 'The Mogarians are after the consignment of precious metals. Got this quaint notion it's been plundered from their planet. They're just recovering stolen property.'

'That can't be your motive,' ventured the Doctor.

'It's greed!' Lasky flung the keys she had gently extricated from the Commodore's pocket at Rudge. She was not intimidated by the volatile situation.

'Not completely,' replied Rudge. 'Pride as well. After this voyage I was being written off as a has-been and put out to grass. I decided to arrange a more comfortable retirement.'

'Pay attention!' The admonition from the loudspeaker was in Atza's guttural tones. 'The *Hyperion III* is no longer under the command of Commodore Travers. He is our prisoner together with three other hostages. All personnel must remain at their posts.'

In the crew's quarters, the pulveriser, the galley, throughout the ship, people had stopped whatever they were doing to listen to Atza's message.

'If there is any attempt to approach the lounge or the bridge, the hostages will be killed!'

The Doctor tousled his hair impatiently. 'Rudge, this hijack's a side show. There's a much greater menace –'

'Not my problem, Doctor,' dismissed his captor. 'In less than an hour, we rendezvous with our pick-up.'

Clutching his wrist, the befuddled Commodore pulled himself upright.

'If you've any decency left, you'll get this man medical treatment,' boomed Lasky, appreciating the intense pain the throbbing, scarlet weal must be causing the Commodore.

'There's a First Aid kit in the cabinet,' Rudge informed the Duty Officer.

'Let me.' The Doctor collected the First Aid kit and crouched beside the Commodore.

Lasky regarded her captor with disgust. 'You're nothing more than a squalid criminal!'

'If I am – what does that make you, Professor?' He was not going to allow this condescending academic to get the better of him. Nor had his small, greedy eyes missed the fact that the Duty Officer had used the exchange to manoeuvre into a position from which he could attack. 'We've already got one wounded hero,' he reminded, menacingly. 'Don't let's add another. Get over there where I can see you.' Despite the bravado, Rudge moved to a wall, protecting his back and distancing himself from his captives.

This provided the opportunity for a hushed conversation between the Commodore and the Doctor.

'What was that performance about?' asked the Commodore quietly as the Doctor dressed his wound. 'In the corridor.'

'To warn Mel. She won't wait around and do nothing. Not in her character.'

Quite true. She had just burst into the communications room intending to send a Mayday call for help.

An abrupt halt. Aghast, she surveyed the wrecked equipment. 'Oh, great!' She turned to her companions. 'Millions of miles from anywhere and we're completely isolated!'

'Can you organise a squad of guards?' Doland asked Janet, his voice echoing as they returned into the long deserted corridor.

'But you heard what the Mogarian said. They'll kill the hostages!' Janet's reluctance aroused Doland's ire.

'What makes you think they won't anyway? You're surely not naïve enough to accept the word of a hijacker!'

'He's right. We can't just do nothing.' Mel's brain was computing the possibilities: the Doctor had to be rescued!

Janet was adamant. 'If the guards go blundering in, they'll be signing four death warrants.'

'Not if we can find a way of warning the hostages . . .' Mel's apprehensive gaze was on the air vent . . .

On the navigational screen, the Black Hole had been replaced by an aspect of distant stars and remote galaxies.

Atza and Ortezo were diligently scanning through a hundred and eighty degrees, seeking another vessel.

The intercom buzzed. Rudge's voice. 'Have you got a sighting yet?'

Switching on his translator, Atza thrust his be-goggled helmet closer to the microphone. 'No. But we are on schedule for our rendezvous. We should complete the mission as planned providing your humans refrain from interference.'

One human, however, was not refraining.

Mel.

On elbows and knees, exuding trepidation lest she bump into a prowling Vervoid, she was squirming along the air duct . . .

'You don't believe Rudge is behind the killings, do you?' The Commodore spoke softly to the Doctor who was bandaging his wound.

'No, he's just a weak man gone rogue.'

'So whatever the outcome of this blasted hijack, we're still at the mercy of a murderer.'

'Or murderers . . .' The Doctor contemplated Lasky.

Sitting apart, reading a book, Sarah Lasky appeared to be in a world of her own.

'Doctor.'

Startled, the Doctor looked about trying to locate the urgent whisper. It sounded like Mel.

'The air duct.' It *was* Mel!

Assuming bored nonchalance in order not to alert Rudge at the far end of the lounge, the Doctor wandered aimlessly towards the air duct. 'What're you doing in there?' He kept his voice very low. 'Don't you know how dangerous it is?'

'Shall I join you!' Whispered it might be, but the tone was tart. 'There's going to be an attack on the lounge. When you hear the fire alarm, dive for cover.'

'No.'

'What d'you mean, no?'

'It's too risky. Attack the bridge.'

'The bridge?'

'You heard! Now get out of that air duct. Quickly!'

She did. But not quickly enough. The occupants on the bridge were about to be attacked. Only not in the way the Doctor would have wanted.

'What are you doing here?' Atza swivelled the command chair as the door slid open. 'We did not request refreshments –'

Before Atza could finish his objection, a shower of liquid was thrown.

But the liquid spraying the Mogarians was neither coffee nor mineral water. It was a corrosive acid that began burning into the material of their protective suits.

Soon each sprinkled droplet became a hole . . .

Exposed to the pernicious, oxygenated air, Atza and Ortezo clutched at their throats . . . and sagged to the deck . . .

21

A Sacrificial Goat

'Not only we kill humankind. They kill each other.' The sibilant conclusions of the First Vervoid hissed around the bulkhead.

Its plant-like confederates nodded bud-shaped heads in agreement with their leader's condemnation. The closely-matted leaves that cloaked their torsos rustled: they were impatient to resume the culling that would eradicate the flawed species.

'Humans have no respect for any form of life,' their self-appointed mentor declared. Then came the edict they were awaiting: 'We shall resume the hunt.'

The Second Vervoid was already en route for its next victim. Crawling along the narrow air duct, it reached the grille in the isolation room and eased its sinewy body through the gap.

Sweeping the black plastic tent apart, the creature's aggressive, irridescent eyes glared with disgust at the travesty on the bed: the pulsating stems laced the smooth skin, and foliage sprouted from the ears of the still recognisably human features.

Rubbery mouth widening with revulsion, the Vervoid thrust its waxy talons at the mutant's throat.

Ruth Baxter's lips separated for a scream that never came . . . the noxious thorn was already embedded in the soft flesh of her neck.

'Death must have been instantaneous. Oxygen's toxic

for a Mogarian,' pronounced Doland.

Mel had relayed the Doctor's instructions to him and Janet. In consequence, they had marshalled several guards who, phasers at the ready, had invaded the bridge.

An abortive mission. The anticipated resistance did not happen. Both Mogarians lay dead.

'Yes, but how?' An irrelevant question. The acid burns on the suits and helmets told Mel how. 'I mean – who could have done this?'

'Forget playing detective! Let's concentrate on the living.' Doland did not want to be drawn into an inquest.

'The hostages?' she asked.

'Rudge has to be convinced the hijack's a lost cause. It'll take more than words.'

A justified observation. Mel had reported that the Security Officer was holding the occupants of the lounge at phaser point.

'Well . . .' Rarely the defeatist, Mel had hit on an idea. She faltered though, not relishing what she was about to suggest. 'Those helmets . . . They'd do the trick . . .'

Assuming command, Doland motioned the guards to remove the Mogarian's helmets.

The faces, when they were unmasked, were a revelation: their classically sculpted features were enhanced by the glowing gold of an unblemished skin. Despite the trauma of their deaths, in final repose Atza's and Ortezo's expressions were aesthetically gentle.

'Mister Rudge, hold your fire we're coming in.'

Entering with hands raised, Mel led the deputation into the lounge.

'The Mogarians are dead,' Janet told him.

Doland did not bother with verbal explanation. He hurled the Mogarian masks at Rudge's feet.

Disbelief chasing astonishment, the Security Officer tried to come to terms with his new predicament. But the element of surprise was sufficient for Doland to chop at the phaser.

It dropped, skittered across the floor, to be seized by the Commodore.

The reversal punctuated Rudge's recently acquired arrogance. Desperately, he shoved Doland into Mel and scarpered. The Duty Officer attempted to give chase.

'Leave him to the guards! Get to the bridge!' The liner was, presumably, on autopilot, but the Commodore wanted no more hitches. 'Now!' he bawled when the Duty Officer did not move fast enough. 'Once I've got this ship back on course, I want some answers!' This was said to the Doctor but Lasky was not spared either. 'And that goes for you, Professor!' Back to the Doctor again: 'A great ally you've proved to be!'

'I haven't been holding out on you. There's an audio tape that will make everything clear.'

'Then why haven't I heard it?' Compromise was not on the Commodore's schedule.

'It's been stolen. I'd like carte blanche to search all cabins.'

'You've got it.' Moving away.

'Another request.'

The Commodore halted.

'I need a phaser.'

Without hesitation, the Commodore thrust Rudge's phaser at the Doctor and quit the lounge.

'A phaser?' Mel had understood that any form of fire-arm was repugnant to the Time Lord.

'Exceptional circumstances call for exceptional measures.'

'I don't buy that.' Compliantly she was allowing him

123

to steer her further away from Lasky and Doland. 'And why the public announcement about the tape? Everyone could hear.'

'Oh, could they?' The fair eyebrows were raised disingenuously.

'I recognise that innocent tone. What's going on?'

'I came into this affair as a Judas goat. I'm readopting the role.' A glance at Lasky. 'Mel, the tape. If Lasky has it, where d'you think she'd hide it?' His speech now was in a lower register.

'Lasky? Her cabin. Or her locker in the gym.'

The locker in the gym was a promising idea, but all Mel found there was the pale blue track suit.

Reluctant to give up that easily, she began searching for any hidden pockets – a hand thumped onto her shoulder!

'If you've finished with my track suit –!' Lasky pursed her mouth to contain her fury.

'I – um – I was admiring the – er – design.'

'Don't bother to lie. You're not very good at it!' Grabbing the suit, she yanked the pockets inside out. 'No tape! That *is* what you were hoping to find, isn't it?'

If Mel's bluff was being called, that was nothing compared with what was happening to Rudge.

Escape was a forlorn dream, but hope is ever present in man's psyche. As Security Officer he was required to know every nook and cranny in the capacious liner: if he could find a hiding place . . . Panting, he descended to the labyrinthine bowels of the vessel and crept through a lower gallery – a Vervoid blocked his way!

He spun about – another Vervoid shuffled from a storeroom.

'What – what are you?'

The hunters began closing in.

'Stay away from me!' Stupefied by the alien sight, Rudge sidled along the wall . . . but in the air duct, a third Vervoid, its staring eyes unblinking, prepared to accept its victim . . .

For Rudge there was to be no escape.

22

Dénouement

The Doctor's search of a suspect's cabin was interrupted by the arrival of its occupant. 'You won't find the tape in there.'

'Does that mean you've hidden it elsewhere?'

'Obviously a denial isn't going to impress you. May I know of what I'm accused?'

'Murder. Among other things.'

'Am I supposed to treat that seriously?'

'I've narrowed the suspects down to two. You and Professor Lasky.'

'Then I suggest you search the Professor's cabin.'

'I already have.'

'You really are serious!'

'I'm never frivolous about murder.'

'And this tape. It's important?'

'Crucial.'

'I see . . . Well, I know I'm innocent. And I can't believe the Professor's guilty. But if it will end this nonsense . . .' A reluctant disclosure. 'There is another place where she keeps her things.'

Scratching his cheek with the phaser, the Doctor indicated Doland to lead the way.

It was to the work hut the pair went. Doland showed him a drawer. But no amount of tugging on the Doctor's part made it budge.

'The Professor's got the only key.'

'And you're not going to object if I force it open.'

Doland shrugged.

Placing the phaser on the bench, the Doctor, using an anti-locking device, opened the drawer and began foraging.

'Don't bother, Doctor.' Doland slid the tape from the pocket of his fawn tabard.

He tossed it, knowing the Doctor would automatically go to catch it. He did – and Doland snatched up the phaser.

Feeling safe now, he smiled. 'Not that the tape'll do you much good. I've wiped it.'

'I rather thought you might have.' The Doctor was remarkably cool.

'You suspected me yet you came down here?'

'A reckless streak I'm prone to.' It had not been difficult to pinpoint Doland. Not once the facts were analysed. 'The first murder had to be committed by someone who had access to this unit.' The reference was to Edwardes' electrocution, the booby trap that had been meant for the inquisitive Mel. 'The second needed poison.' He indicated the bottles and flasks, any of which could have contained the poison administered to Hallet. 'Even the abortive attempt on Mel's life could only have been carried out by someone able to go unchallenged into the isolation room to get the anaesthetic.'

'All of which could have applied to Lasky.'

'Not the Mogarians. She was a hostage when they were slaughtered.'

The concise and correct summing up came as stale news to Doland.

Not to another listener though.

At the air duct in the cargo hold, peering from an angle just acute enough to bring the two men into view, were the baleful, vermilion features of the Second Vervoid.

'And my motive?' Gone was the subservience.

Doland's feeling of superiority was vested in his possession of the phaser.

'Could have been jealousy. Professional envy. But I'd say it's the more commonplace avarice.'

'Then you're not as astute as I thought. These creatures – we call them Vervoids – represent economic power.'

'Providing you can deliver them to Earth.'

'Oh, but I will. No matter what the cost.' Like many criminals, Doland was unable to resist boasting: vanity required that ingenuity and cleverness be accorded their accolade. The scientist was being afforded his moment of glory in complete security: the Doctor would be dead before he could alert the authorities. Triumph made him expansive. 'Then robots can be dumped on the scrap heap. Vervoids will run factories and farms at practically no cost. All they need is sunlight and water.'

'I take it you have allies willing to finance this exploitation.'

'A consortium with the vision to see the potential of the Vervoids.'

'Vision! You're talking about slave labour!'

'The most enduring and spectacular empire – Rome – was built on slave labour.'

'Came to an unpleasant end though.'

'Which brings us neatly to you.' He fired the phaser.

A click. Nothing more.

He fired again.

Same result.

'I took the precaution of disarming it.'

A prerequisite of murder is an inflated conceit – a belief in one's inviolability. Disbelief jockeying with reality, Doland glared at the Doctor: how could this buffoon have outwitted him?

Enraged at being duped, he slung the useless phaser

at the Time Lord and ran from the hut – into an implacable squad of guards fronted by the Commodore!

'I also took the precaution of taking the Commodore into my confidence.' Under cover of accepting the phaser, the Doctor had slipped a warning note to the Commodore after their rescue in the lounge.

'Throw him in the brig!'

Flanked by his escort, Doland was despondent. The section they were negotiating was dimly lit and spartan.

'Catacombs!' he thought, bitterly: an apt setting for his shattered ambitions. But the delinquent scientist would have regarded the brig as a safe haven had he known what really lay in wait.

The ambush, when it was sprung, was swift and grimly efficient.

Forced into single file by a restricted aisle, the armed guards were despatched by the lurking Vervoids with dispassionate ease. Not expecting attack, and awe-struck by the grotesque nature of their asssailants, the unfortunate men failed even to unholster their weapons before the lethal thorns felled them.

The sole survivor, Doland found himself confronted by the Second Vervoid. Escape was not a possibility: the operation had been co-ordinated. Having executed the first stage, the rest of the Vervoids completed the second. He was encircled.

'No! Stop! I'm not your enemy!' Doland's innate opportunism reasserted itself. 'Without me you wouldn't exist.' He gazed imploringly at each bud-shaped head framed by an ivory-brown corolla, seeking a hint of expression.

There was none. Even the eyes were impassive.

The scientist's vanity rejected defeat: these Vervoids were his creation and, therefore, of inferior intellect. 'There is so much more I could do for you.' He relaxed.

The ploy had worked. The Second Vervoid was extending its hand.

Suffused by a warm glow of relief, Doland clasped the waxy, leaf-veined fingers in a seal of mutual friendship.

But his confident grin wavered into uncertainty as he released his grasp . . . sticking into his moist palm was a thorn.

Through the dismal mist of approaching death, the final sentence the murderer, Doland heard was:

'Vervoids will never be enslaved . . .'

23

Philosophy of a Vervoid

'You created these psychopaths. Now tell me how to get rid of them!' On the bridge, the Commodore swung his command chair towards Lasky. His outburst was merited. Spurred on by their mounting pile of corpses, the Vervoids were attacking at will. Corridors and cabins became death-traps for the unwary.

'The Vervoids are not psychopaths.'

'Doctor, I heard them declare they intended to wipe us out,' averred Mel.

Lasky was still seeking a rationale. 'Something must have gone wrong. Radically wrong. A malfunction involving the DNA –'

'Why is it none of you can see what's so glaringly obvious?' interrupted the Doctor.

'Maybe we lack your divine insight!' came the Commodore's sarcastic retort.

'I've no divine insight. Only logic.'

'Logic?'

'Mel, when you overheard the Vervoids, how did they describe us?'

'Um . . . wait a sec . . . animalkind.'

'Not human. Not Mogarian. Animalkind.'

The Doctor's dissertation had already lost the Commodore. 'I hope this is relevant.'

'It is,' Lasky conceded. 'He's making sense. The Vervoids are plants.'

'At some stage and in some form, all animal kind consumes plant life. Without it we'd perish.' The

Doctor's argument was irrefutable.

'I must have been blinded by professional vanity. Bruchner saw it. I should have too.' Arrogance came naturally to Lasky but humility would describe her emotions now.

'If you're right, Doctor . . . co-existence with Vervoids is an impossibility . . .' Trust Mel not to equivocate.

The Commodore, too, recognised the impasse. 'So it's down to self-preservation. Kill or be killed.'

'A conflict in which there can be no justice.' Deep ridges furrowed the Doctor's brow as he uttered this sad conclusion.

'Equally, there's no choice!' The Commodore was resolute. 'And that goes for you as well, Doctor. We need your undivided commitment!'

*   *   *

'And there you have it! The direct request!' The Doctor's declaration accompanied the conclusive flourish with which he flicked off the Matrix screen. 'I did not meddle. I was presented with an appeal. Not simply from an individual – but from the man in whom authority was vested!'

'I accept the argument. Nor, Valeyard, can you refute it.'

The Inquisitor's decision should have deflated the Valeyard's ego. It did not! 'Perhaps before we reach a verdict, Eminence, we should await the outcome of the adventure.' Moderation oozed from every pore. 'Shall we continue?'

'Do you wish to continue?' the Inquisitor asked.

The Doctor was troubled by the enigmatic stance of his prosecutor. He had scored the vital point in his own defence, yet the Valeyard was obviously not displeased.

Only one explanation suggested itself.

'Yes, my Lady. Providing we can trust the Matrix. I won't know that until I see it . . .' Apprehensively he switched on.

*　　*　　*

Professor Lasky held an empty bottle upside down. 'There's not enough left to make a spoonful of herbicide!'

The Doctor had suggested that the Vervoids could be destroyed by the effects of a strong herbicide. But the Vervoids not only had the ability to move and speak like humans, they also had the ability to think. They had anticipated this eventuality and emptied every carboy of its contents.

Lasky knew they would have been capable of such a deduction. 'The Vervoids got here first!'

'Any more ideas, Doctor?' Mel's hopes were firmly vested in the Time Lord.

'Why can't I rid myself of the feeling we're approaching this the wrong way round?' Posing the hypothetical question, the Doctor led Mel and Lasky from the work hut past the discarded shucks which were beginning to fade and turn brown. The notice –
HIGH INTENSITY LIGHT FORBIDDEN. LOW SPECTRUM LIGHT ONLY – still prominently displayed, now served no purpose.

Or did it . . .? The Doctor arrested his progress. 'Do Vervoid chloroplasts function normally?'

Thrown by the abrupt change of tack, Lasky parried the remark. 'A cytogeneticist now! You're a man of varied talents.'

'Don't prevaricate, Professor!' The Doctor was excited.

'Yes. Vervoid chloroplasts trap sunlight as is normal

with all plants.'

'Doctor!' cried Mel. 'There's something out there!'

Congregating in the hold, lidless eyes probing the gloom, thorny talons flexing, a pack of Vervoids was converging on the trio . . .

'Is there another exit?' the Doctor asked Lasky.

'Not this side of the hold.'

Leaves rustling, the Vervoids had effectively hemmed them in.

Grabbing the two women, the Doctor retreated to the mesh fence. Lasky shrugged him off. 'No. I'm going to talk to them.'

The Doctor stopped. 'They won't listen, Professor!'

Lasky was adamant. 'Perhaps they will. To me.'

'It's too much of a risk!' He recognised that instinct not sentimentality was motivating the creatures.

'I wasn't going to exploit them like Doland. They'll know that.'

'Doctor! Professor! Come on!' Indefatigable as ever, Mel had managed to find an air vent. 'Come on!'

Torn between Lasky's heroic foolhardiness and his own salvation, the Time Lord made a last despairing appeal. 'They'll spare no one!'

'I have to try.' Resolutely she walked forward.

For Sarah Lasky the gathering crisis threatening to engulf them was not simply a matter of survival: she could contemplate death without lapsing into palsied fear. No, her distress sprang from more profound origins: her extrovert hauteur was an armour protecting the exposed nerve ends of a sensitive nature.

She had modelled her style on her father: a celebrated scientist accorded recognition and esteem. It was a posture that cost her dearly. Throughout her adult life, she never formed a close relationship and everybody who came into contact with her assumed she was utterly self-contained.

The only person who could have corrected that mistaken assumption died when Sarah was twelve years old – her mother. Hubert Lasky had ruled by the oppressive weight of intellectual dominance, but it was her frail and delicate mother to whom Sarah was devoted.

Mother and daughter shared a secret. One which would have aroused scathing contempt from the father had he ever learnt of it. Yet, with hindsight, it was unfortunate that he did not; for the secret set Sarah on the path leading to the Vervoid nightmare. The innocent confidence the two shared was that the mother talked, in gentle coaxing tones, to her house plants. She was convinced that indoor azaleas, fuchsias, and petunias responded to the warmth of affection.

While still devastated by the bleakness following the loss of her mother, the acutely shy Sarah read of a discovery in the late twentieth century by a French biochemist, Ladzunski, that a vital hormone essential to the functioning of the human brain also acts as a signal molecule in plants.

Intolerable paternal pressure ensured Sarah became a scientist, apparently treading in her father's hallowed footsteps. In truth, she continued to walk with the only person with whom she had enjoyed happiness and understanding. The sad irony was that such blameless fidelity should have spawned the creatures now confronting her.

'You must know who I am.'

'Yes, Professor Lasky, we do.' The Second Vervoid acted as intermediary.

'Then you must also be aware I mean you no harm.'

Vulnerability was not an adjective that would have seemed apt in a biography of Sarah Lasky, but dwarfed and surrounded by the predatory Vervoids, there could be no more poignant a description. Whether she was driven by bravado or belief, her bold, blue eyes exhibited no fear.

'All animalkind is our enemy, Professor.' The Second Vervoid's rebuttal was unconditional. 'Even you.'

Gently, the nearest Vervoid lifted Sarah Lasky's blonde hair . . . then flicked a thorn into the nape of her neck . . . The delicacy with which the thorn was embedded may have hinted at a trace of regret . . . but the result of the venom was just as deadly.

Vervoid philosophy recognised no exceptions . . .

24

The Life Cycle

Mel saw them first.

'Don't – don't come in here . . .'

But the Doctor had already seen the sorry collection of bodies. Crawling through the ducts in their escape from the cargo hold, they had entered the bulkhead and stumbled upon the improvised cage.

A sob escaped Mel's throat. 'How could they?' Her words were muffled as the Doctor swung her into his shoulder. 'How could they! It's obscene!'

'Not to a Vervoid, Mel.' He spoke soothingly, understanding the distress of his young companion. Yet he, with the superior intellect and empathy of a Time Lord, was able to encompass more than the narrow angle of a human viewpoint.

'You can't justify it! They're ghouls! Nothing but ghouls!'

'It's a matter of perspective, Mel,' he coaxed. 'In Pease Pottage you had a very large garden.'

She gazed at him uncomprehendingly.

'What did you do with the weeds and plants you uprooted?'

'Put them on a compost heap . . .' her voice took on a dying fall as comprehension began to dawn.

'They're obeying instinct. Like migrating birds.' While speaking, he stared at the lamp which was the bulkhead's sole illumination. 'Or the salmon swimming relentlessly upstream to breed even though they may perish. A compulsive following of the life cycle.'

He held his palm close to the lamp.

An idea was forming in the Doctor's mind . . .

The death of Lasky appeared to have added impetus to the warfare.

Vervoids roamed the ship.

Corridors became no-go areas.

Passengers collected in groups, locking themselves in cabins in the vain hope they would be spared. Nowhere was safe.

Swiping wildly with a metal scoop, the operator in the waste disposal unit was keeping a Vervoid at bay. He scored a direct hit that toppled his gangling foe into a wastebin.

With frenzied speed, the operator slammed the bin against the pulveriser . . . and the waxy, green creature was sucked into its chomping jaws.

But the victor's moment of triumph was fleeting. The assailant had not been alone. Another Vervoid, armed with a phaser captured from a guard, fired . . .

In the lounge, recliners and tables were being stacked to barricade the door against a mounted attack.

Despite the efforts of Janet and the guards to keep it secure, the blockade was shifting inexorably.

'It's useless, Commodore,' Janet wailed into the communicator. 'They're everywhere. We –'

'– can't hope to defeat them!'

'Yes we can!' Striding onto the bridge, the Doctor heard Janet's plaintive cry over the intercom. 'With your help, Commodore.'

'Name it!'

'Like the Vervoids, we're being driven by instinct. Kill or be killed.'

'We've been over that!'

'What if instead of bringing our lives to an abrupt end, we did the opposite? Accelerated the Vervoid life cycle?'

'How the blazes can we do that?'

'Vionesium.'

'Vionesium?' repeated Mel, making her presence felt.

'A rare metal found on the airless planet of Mogar,' explained the Doctor.

'And worth a prince's ransom.'

'Or a hijack . . .' suggested the Doctor significantly.

'You mean there's a consignment on board?'

'That's right,' the Commodore affirmed to Mel. 'In the vault.'

'But how will this vionesium accelerate the Vervoid life cycle?' Mel was no biologist.

'It's a substance similar to magnesium. Exposed to oxygenated air, it releases incredibly intense sunlight and carbon dioxide. Spring, summer, autumn all condensed into moments.'

The Doctor's enthusiasm was not wholeheartedly shared by the Commodore. 'Seasons which I may be a long time enjoying again if I go on robbing my own vault!'

'Seasons you can forget if you don't!' The 'compost heap' of bodies had left Mel with absolutely no illusions. 'We've seen what these creatures do to humans.'

'I don't think you've an alternative, Commodore.' The Doctor opted for persuasion rather than pressure.

'Sending for outside help's not on. The ship's completely cut off.' Mel's pale face looked strained as she urged the Commodore to accept. 'The Doctor's the only hope you've got . . .'

The Commodore capitulated. 'All right, Doctor. What's the drill?'

'First you must get the Vervoids to return to their

lair.'

'Me? How?'

'Put the ship in darkness. . . .'

The barricade in the lounge bar was in danger of being breached when the lights flickered.

'Attention!' The stern directive rasping from the loudspeaker caused a lull in the assault.

'Attention all passengers and crew. A major fault had developed in the generators.' The lights dimmed perceptibly.

'To effect necessary repairs, the heating will be shut down.' Listening to the loudspeaker in the gym, a Vervoid hastily unclamped the grille to retreat into the air vent.

'Auxiliary lighting only will be in operation.'

Deck after deck plunged into darkness. Even the soft glow of exhaust heat emissions was quenched as the majestic *Hyperion III* lost all power.

The great liner hovered motionlessly in space like a ghost ship: an inert hulk vaguely silhouetted against remote galaxies, giving no hint of the titanic conflict reaching a climax within its beleaguered shell.

The outcome of this conflict would have repercussions for millions of beings who were unaware that their fate depended on the sagacity of a slightly eccentric Time Lord.

Cramped, a tension cleat chafing his hip, the Doctor pressed into a recess behind a stanchion. Discomfort was not his principal worry. The Vervoids trailing into their bulkhead lair were. It was imperative that the Duty Officer and Mel remained undetected until they got into position.

'Are we all here?' asked the Second Vervoid.

'One of us has been destroyed, but there is still another to come.'

'This power fault could be a trick.' Suspicion was a singular trait of the Second Vervoid's personality.

'What can they gain?' reasoned the First Vervoid. 'Animalkind need the life support system. They must repair the generators to survive.'

Sceptically, the Second Vervoid peered into the sepulchral outer reaches of the bulkhead.

Lying prone in a gulley housing a swollen pipe, the Duty Officer was well-concealed. But Mel, hiding in an inlet, eased nervously into the shadows.

Mel glanced at the golden capsule of vionesium she clutched. Each of them had a similar golden capsule: three in all. A shiver of fear trembled through her slender frame: if the Doctor's plan failed, her life would surely be forfeit. How many short months had elapsed since she had inhabited the secure purlieus of Pease Pottage where keeping abreast of the rapid changes in computer hardware was the greatest challenge?

A sinister rustling from the rear brought her back to the present. The latecomer was shuffling towards the lair via the duct in which Mel had taken shelter.

The Second Vervoid, already disquieted, moved swiftly to investigate the rustling. An action that convinced Mel she would be trapped between the two creatures.

Allowing panic to dictate her response, she scrambled from the inlet.

With contemptuous nonchalance, the tall, plantoid Vervoids formed a towering barrier about the diminutive human specimen now rooted to the spot in quivering paralysis.

'The vionesium, Mel!' the Doctor bawled.

Jolted from her stupor, she fumbled with the catch on the golden capsule.

Abandoning cover, the Doctor flipped open his capsule and lobbed its contents into the midst of the Vervoids. On cue, the Duty Officer did the same.

The distraction gave Mel the opportunity to open her capsule.

Three sticks of vionesium hit the ground, instantaneously flaring into brilliant white light.

Bedazzled Vervoids tried to shield their eyes . . . but the pulsating flares encircled the hapless creatures. Disorientated, they reeled helplessly, moaning in pain: a *danse macabre* whose descant was the eerie ululations.

Haloed against the harsh incandescent light, the Second Vervoid loomed over Mel – but the Doctor, risking his own safety, grabbed her by the scruff of the neck and dragged her into the darkness fringing the bulkhead.

Pulsating, wavering shadows from the lair were thrown across Mel and the Doctor as the Time Lord's prognosis was realised. The leaves on the Vervoids' torsos were no longer olive-green. Instead they were changing to autumn yellow.

Mel clamped her hands over her ears to block out the melancholy lament.

Throughout the ship, on the bridge, in the lounge, the crew's quarters, the plaintive requiem could be heard, permeating an overwhelming sense of sadness.

A sadness that afflicted the Doctor. In the lair, the leaves decayed to a russet brown and, curling, began to fall to the ground. The ululations declined into senile whimpers. Soon even the vines that formed the Vervoid skeletons withered and dropped.

Silence.

All that remained of the Vervoids was a carpet of dried, brittle leaves and twigs. . . .

Releasing Mel, the Doctor picked up a leaf – it crumbled to dust in his palm . . . From his pocket he took a communicator:

'You can restore power, Commodore . . . It's over . . .'

The TARDIS was a welcome sight for Mel. She and the Doctor were preparing to leave.

Janet and Commodore Travers had come to bid them farewell: on his part not so much a gesture of politeness as a desire to make certain the Time Lord actually left!

'*Au revoir*,' said the pretty stewardess.

The Commodore grinned ruefully. 'Not *au revoir*! I owe you my thanks, Doctor, but let's make this the "sweet sorrow" of a final parting!'

'I'll remember that the next time we get a Mayday call,' quipped Mel, smiling.

'And she's not joking!' The Doctor looked down at his petite companion. 'Memory like an elephant.'

'That's his idea of a compliment, comparing me with an elephant.'

'It's so ludicrously inappropriate, I find it funny.' The Doctor's face creased with delight.

'Well, at least if you're laughing you can't be singing!' Mel mocked. 'Ever heard his rendering of *On With The Motley*?'

Amused, the Commodore shook his head.

'Count your blessings! Come on, Doctor!'

Grabbing the initiative, she pushed him inside the TARDIS.

But she had already initiated a train of thought. Above the familiar wheezing of dematerialisation, the strains of the operatic aria could be heard being sung in the Doctor's own inimitable style.

Mel had brought that punishment on herself!

Epilogue

'None of the unfortunate creatures survived, Doctor?'

The Matrix screen had been switched off as the TARDIS dematerialised.

'No, my Lady. Had even a leaf survived and fallen on fertile soil, a Vervoid would have grown.'

'Every Vervoid was destroyed by your ingenious ploy?' Was there a hint of suppressed excitement beneath the Valeyard's guileless question?

The Doctor hesitated before replying: he was perturbed by the seeming complacency. 'Yes . . .'

Barely able to conceal his triumph, the Valeyard rose to address the Court. 'Whether or not the Doctor has proved himself innocent of meddling is no longer the cardinal issue before this Court,' came the sonorous tones. 'He has proved himself guilty of a far greater crime.'

The Doctor's ruddy face blanched.

'You refer to Article Seven of Gallifreyan Law?' The Inquisitor's voice was grave.

'No! No! That cannot apply!' protested the Doctor. 'Had the Vervoids reached Earth, the human race would have been eliminated! Or – at best – banished to the barren deserts or the Arctic wastes!'

Valeyard was unrelenting. 'My Lady, Article Seven permits no exceptions. The Doctor has destroyed an entire species.' Dramatically, he faced the accused. 'The charge must now be genocide . . .'